CUA

Run for Home

Run for Home

DAN LATUS

ROBERT HALE · LONDON

ISBN 978-0-7198-1071-8

Robert Hale Limited
Clerkenwell House
Clerkenwell Green
London EC1R 0HT

www.halebooks.com

2 4 6 8 10 9 7 5 3 1

Typeset in New Century Schoolbook
Printed in the UK by the Berforts Group

For the girls: Hazel, Emily and Megan

Chapter One

A flash of light that shouldn't have happened caught his eye. He blinked but kept going. Further along the pavement, he slowed and stepped sideways into the doorway of a Chinese grocery store.

He moved deep inside, amongst the half-dozen customers, and considered his options: to go on, or to abort? He wasn't sure.

He took a jar of pickled cabbage from a shelf and turned to examine the vegetable racks stacked near the door. From there, he could see the third-floor window in the apartment building across the street. It was in darkness.

He waited a minute or two, foraging amongst the pods of broad beans and the cabbages, but he didn't see another flash of light. Had he imagined it?

No. He was sure he hadn't. As ever, he had been vigilant on his approach to the safe house. It paid to be careful, and caution was second nature to him anyway.

If the others had arrived, as they should have done by now, the light would have been on in the room; it wasn't. He could think of nothing that might have caused a brief flash of light, nothing normal at least. It was worrying.

He came to a decision and chose several large sweet

potatoes to present to the small, tired woman behind the counter. She gave him a token smile, and weighed and bagged them, together with the jar of pickled cabbage. He paid and returned her courteous *Na'sledenou!* Goodbye!

Coming out of the shop, he turned to his right without looking up and walked purposefully along the street. Autumn, going on for winter. The last of the daylight almost gone now. There were deep shadows in doorways and stairwells. He breathed in the dank seasonal smell, and the breath he exhaled hung in a small cloud on the air before his face. Car headlights dazzled as they approached and swept past.

The flash of light still bothered him, made him uneasy, and he stayed on full alert. But he detected nothing else out of the ordinary. No one seemed to be watching the apartment building from any of the doorways he passed; no one was hanging around seemingly with nothing to do. There were no parked or idling cars on this section of the street. Everything looked normal. But he couldn't get past the thought that the flash of light wasn't normal. There was no obvious reason for it.

At the next intersection, he waited until a tram had squealed to a stop and then he dodged behind it and crossed the road, using the opportunity to glance upwards and to his left. The window was in darkness.

Back on pavement again, he dropped the bag of sweet potatoes and pickled cabbage into a bin and walked at a leisurely pace back towards the entrance to the building. When he reached it, he turned and climbed the half-dozen stone steps to the front door. He took his time. No hurry. A weary man heading home after his day's work, perhaps? But his antennae were bristling, on guard for anything the slightest out of the ordinary.

The lighting in the hallway was dim; economy lighting,

not much better than emergency lighting. Paradoxically, the building was overheated, as if, unlike light, heat came free. So always, when they met here, they opened the window wide as soon as they arrived. He had seen it wasn't open today. Something else to worry about.

Were the others not here yet? It didn't look like it. Odd. He was slightly late himself. Were they later still?

He stood still in the entrance hall and listened. He heard the rattle of the heating pipes and the gurgling of an ancient radiator. Somewhere a door slammed shut, the sound reverberating. There were children's voices upstairs, and he heard children's feet clattering along a stone-floored corridor. He turned his head slightly and listened to the traffic noise building up outside, as evening set in. Then the lift began to whine as it started its slow, cranky descent.

He walked briskly a dozen paces along the dimly lit corridor to his left. Then he stopped and turned to face a scarred wooden door, his finger poised ready to press the buzzer set in the wall alongside.

The lift stopped and he heard its cage door rattle open. Moments later two men walked past the end of the corridor, heading towards the exit from the building. He waited until he heard the front door slam shut. Then he waited a few moments longer – an old precaution – before pressing the buzzer.

As the door to the apartment opened, he glimpsed out of the corner of his eye a figure appear at the end of the corridor. He didn't turn to look but he knew one of the men had turned back, and that he was being observed. He didn't like that. The dim light gave him some protection, his fur hat and upturned coat collar rather more, but it wasn't good to be under inspection.

The tired and middle-aged woman who had come to the door looked up at him expectantly with a polite smile. He asked for Pán Novotny, having seen the name on a slip of card housed in the small tin bracket to one side of the door.

'He is not here yet,' the woman said. 'May I help you?'

He shook his head, sighed and launched into a complicated fiction. They – his company – had been contacted by her husband, he said, about thermostatic radiator valves. He was anxious to progress matters.

No, she replied, shaking her head. It couldn't have been her husband. He expressed surprise. She was sure? She was sure. He was astonished, couldn't believe it. But she was certain.

She was so sure, she said, because they had already had such valves fitted. In these old flats you needed them. Otherwise the windows had to be open all the time, it was so hot. She knew she shouldn't complain about being too hot in winter, but really. . . .

It was true, he said. He understood the problem. It was why his company. . . . He stopped, sighed with exasperation and proffered his apologies. He was so sorry to have disturbed her. The people in the office! Wasting both his time and hers.

She nodded and sympathized. It was still like that, everywhere. One day it would be different perhaps, even for ordinary people like them. Better, even. Her husband thought so. For herself, she wasn't so sure. After all, twenty years had passed already, she added with a shrug of resignation as she started to close the door.

When he turned away, the figure at the end of the corridor was no longer there. He walked back to the hall, satisfied himself that no one was lurking, and headed for the stairs.

He didn't trust lifts. These lifts, especially. They were open cages, traps, and inclined to fail and strand you helpless.

No one was about in the corridor on the third floor. He walked quickly along to the second door on the left and pressed the buzzer. He heard the raw sound of it reverberate inside the flat. No one came to the door. After a few moments, he used his key to open the door and stepped inside.

The sweet smell struck him instantly. He grimaced with recognition. Holding his breath, he moved reluctantly into the main room, his heart pounding.

They were there, the others. All three of them. None were alive. They had been shot in the back of the head: execution style. And not long ago. Their bodies were still warm.

There wasn't much blood, but what there was he had identified as soon as he had opened the door. That distinctive, sickening smell you never forgot, and never mistook for anything else.

Shot. He knew now what had caused the flash of light. Landis had taken more than one bullet. He had tried to reach the window, perhaps to warn him. If so, it had worked.

Gregory and Phillips, meanwhile, had died as they had lived – quietly.

He swore savagely. He was shocked, and sickened. He fought back a wave of nausea. The questions were racing through his mind but he resisted them. He knew he couldn't allow himself to be distracted. Survival, his own, was the priority now.

He had been lucky – so far. If he hadn't been late arriving, there would have been four corpses here, not three. And if he didn't get away quickly there still might be. He grimaced again, knowing he might already have made a mistake in turning on the lights as he entered the flat.

There was nothing to be done here. He turned to leave, and then checked. There was something here he could use, and might well need now it had come to this.

It took seconds to lift the floorboard and take out the holdall where the money in different currencies was kept, much of it in high-denomination banknotes. He had no idea how much there was; Landis had never said. But the weight told him it was a lot. Better for it to go with him than be left here. He also took out a handgun, a Glock pistol, and a box of ammunition.

He closed the door to the flat quietly when he left and walked quickly along to the central stairwell. Even before he got there he heard soft feet on the staircase down below. More than one person coming up, moving fast. He turned and ran upwards himself, quickly but quietly, staying close to the wall.

On the next floor, he hurried along the corridor to the far end, burst through the emergency door and ran down the metal fire-escape, down the four flights to the yard at the back of the building and out into a narrow alleyway. Then he walked quickly back to his car, parked several blocks away in a side street, and got into it with mixed feelings of relief and shock. Despair and anger, too.

He leant forward, closed his eyes and pressed his forehead hard against the steering wheel for a moment.

All of them. Damn, damn, damn! All three.

He straightened up. His inclination was to get as far away as possible, as quickly as he could, but he couldn't do that. Not yet.

He started the engine, drove back along the main street and parked on a small patch of vacant land next to the railway, alongside several other cars. From there, he could see the entrance to the building.

It was a busy corner. The traffic streamed by incessantly. Cars and a few trams, all ablaze with light now dusk had given way to night. People hurried along on foot, their breath clouding the air. Behind him a long goods train moved past slowly at the foot of the Vyšehrad hill, heading for the tunnel and then the bridge over the Vltava.

For ten minutes, nothing out of the ordinary happened across the street. He was shivering continually by then. It was bitterly cold and difficult to sit still, especially after what he had just discovered. Difficult to concentrate, as well. He began to think he should just go, after all – leave, get out, while he still could.

Then a shiny black car, a Jaguar, pulled up outside the building and sat with its lights on and the engine running, wisps of condensation and fumes puffing into the evening air. Two men in leather jackets came out of the building. At the foot of the steps, they paused to light cigarettes before getting into the car, which immediately pulled away fast into the traffic stream.

He was stunned and dismayed. Jackson and Murphy? Surely not! But it was. He was in no doubt whatsoever.

So he had something else to think about now. He swore bitterly and started the engine. Time he was gone.

Chapter Two

'It's done.'

'All of them?'

'Well. . . .' Jackson hesitated and glanced sideways at his partner, Murphy, with a grimace. 'Actually. . . .'

'All of them?' the boss man insisted.

'All but one.'

In the silence that followed, Jackson waited patiently. He knew there might be an explosion of rage. He would just have to weather it. Fortunately, it was a telephone conversation, not a face-to-face meeting.

'Presumably one got away?'

He breathed easily again. 'One wasn't there. Just three of them.'

Another lengthy pause. Thinking time. Jackson waited, and motioned to Murphy to keep quiet.

'So which one was missing?'

He told him.

Then there was an explosion, but it was not particularly directed at him and Murphy. It was more a matter of frustration with the world in general.

He held on until the man calmed down and told him what

to do next. Then he said yes, they would, and put the phone down. It clattered off the rest and fell to the floor. Damned old-fashioned thing! But they had to use them. Mobiles were too insecure.

'What did he say?' Murphy asked.

'In a nutshell?'

'That will do.'

'He said to find him – and finish the job.'

Murphy nodded. 'No surprise there. We knew it would come to this.'

Jackson agreed.

'Did he say where to start?'

Jackson grinned, but without being amused. 'I did ask him, but he just said it was down to us. That was what we were being paid for.'

'Like that, eh?' Murphy said with a chuckle.

'Like that.'

Murphy switched on the TV. Jackson watched him do it, but he couldn't be bothered with television himself. There was too much to think about, and even more to do.

Chapter Three

He left Prague just before ten that night, crossed the Channel twelve hours later and got there early the next evening. He knew he was 'there' because it felt right. Not the end of the line perhaps, but the end of his journey. For now. There would be other journeys to come but he needed rest, and he needed time to think.

He parked in the main street and switched off the ignition. Then he sat quietly for a while with his eyes closed, listening to the clicks and creaks of the hard-pressed engine getting used to being at rest at last.

By the time he got out of the car, the light had gone altogether. Late October. What could you expect? He locked the door and turned to look up and down the street.

Not much was happening. One elderly man was walking his dog. Two others were standing talking, leaning against the iron railings at a bus stop. He saw two middle-aged women, arm in arm, walking quickly on the other side of the road, and three teenage kids locked in animated conversation as they unhurriedly crossed the road. A couple of cars crept past, and then a giant truck carrying logs swept through as if confident it had absolute right of way. Another followed close behind.

It was just a village. Quiet. Peaceful. And, he dared to hope, safe for the moment. With luck, he would be able to get something to eat and some sleep before he moved on.

They had a spare room in the only hotel – just a pub, really – which was on the main street. The Running Man. He wasn't sure about the name. It was a bit too close to home. But he took the room anyway. Any port in a storm. It was no time to be fussy.

The hotel had any amount of spare rooms, was his guess. Not many customers in the bar, and he was the only one in the dining room. He was soon served with a meal. Lamb cutlets and winter vegetables, followed by coffee. He scarcely knew what he was eating, he was so tired. He was exhausted.

The woman that seemed to run the place came to refill his coffee cup and have a word with him about breakfast.

'Breakfast?' he repeated dully.

She smiled. 'That's right. It's the first meal of the day around here.'

He tried to smile back.

'So what would you like?'

'Anything,' he said.

'Bacon and egg? Full English? Continental? What's your fancy?'

He shook his head. Breakfast seemed too far ahead.

'Do I need to decide now?'

'No, of course not.' She smiled again. 'I can see you're very tired. Don't worry. We'll sort it out in the morning.'

He nodded, grateful to her for finding a solution.

'I'm Ellie, by the way. If you want anything, just ask for me.'

She seemed a nice woman, he thought, as he watched her retreat towards the kitchen. Pretty, as well. Good figure, and he'd always liked shoulder-length dark hair. He wondered if she did everything around here. It seemed as if she did. So far, she had booked him in, shown him to his room, served him dinner, asked him what he wanted for breakfast. . . . There wasn't much else left to do.

He smiled wryly to himself. Multitasking! Wasn't that what they called it?

Afterwards, he went up to his room, lay on the bed and tried to think things through. A lot had happened in twenty-four hours, and he doubted if it had finished yet. But at least he had got out. Somehow he had. For now, he was fairly safe.

They would look for him, of course. He was sure of that. Something had happened, obviously. Whatever it was, they wouldn't want a loose cannon like him roaming around. Take him out as well. That would be the plan. It had to be. Nothing else made sense.

Initially, he had assumed the opposition had got to the others, careful though they had always been about their meetings. But as soon as he had seen Jackson and Murphy, he had known the truth: they were cleaners, two of the best – if not *the* best. They swept things up and tidied them away. People, included. And bodies. So it wasn't the Russians, after all. It was his own side.

Why, though? He scowled and shook his head. It was a fucking nightmare! He had no idea why. None at all. So far as he knew, nothing out of the ordinary had happened. Landis had called a special meeting, but it wasn't as if it was the first time that had happened. From time to time, they did need to get together.

It wouldn't be happening again, though. It struck him then that Unit 89 had effectively ceased to exist. Three dead and him on the run. It was almost as if it had never been.

Could that be the plan, the reason? Make their team not only deniable but non-existent, a figment of the imagination?

He shook his head. He had no idea. Anyway, the why of it didn't really matter right now. Not to him. What he needed to do was focus on protecting himself. And Lisa. Always Lisa.

He wondered if they would find him. Hard to say. But he knew it was possible. He had stuck a pin in his mental road atlas and covered a lot of ground to get here, this place he didn't know and had no previous connection with; but randomness wasn't everything. No guarantees came with it. He would just have to be careful, and avoid slip-ups. Otherwise, Lisa. . . .

He shuddered. Best not to think of her right now, hard as it was. Or Landis and the others either. Keep things simple. Do the best he could, and hope it worked out.

He opened the holdall Landis had kept stored beneath the floorboards and stared at the money. He shook his head. Then he started counting it, which was something he had not dared to take time out to do until now; he had just grabbed it and run. There was ample, he soon decided, more than enough for the foreseeable future. He stopped counting and zipped up the bag.

There might be even more money, if he needed it. He knew where there was an emergency fund. Electronic banking, though? He grimaced. Activity could be monitored, and it left traces. Anyway, why bother? Money was the least of his worries right now.

He really would need to be careful, if he wanted to live – which he did. Very much so. Mostly for Lisa and himself. But he also wanted the chance to hit back. He owed it to the others not to take this lying down. They had always been one for all, and all for one. In their line of work, you couldn't operate entirely alone. You depended on a handful of people, and they became important to you. He wasn't going to forget them now.

He shook his head and yawned. God, he was tired! He wondered about sleeping just as he was, fully dressed. But some of the fear and the urgency had left him now. He felt secure enough to risk undressing. Besides, he needed to look after himself – and his clothes, until he could buy more – to avoid attracting attention. He got up off the bed, undressed and took a shower. After that he could put off sleep no longer.

In the morning he didn't feel so good. He had slept, off and on, but he hadn't been able to escape the horrors. Back from exhaustion, he was on edge again – hyper. He got up as soon as it was light and stood beside his window. Easing the curtain slightly aside with one finger, he checked that his car was still there. Then he studied the street.

There were plenty of people about. They were all moving purposefully, walking dogs or heading for their work or their morning paper. No one was just standing, watching and waiting, in the shadows. Still, why would they be? He shrugged and let the curtain go, and turned away from the window to get washed and dressed.

This place had been good for him but his mind was made up. He would get moving again. Movement might not solve anything but he needed it. An illusion, perhaps, but he wanted the feeling of being in control that movement gave him.

He wasn't hungry and declined the offer of a full English. He just wanted enough calories to put something back into the fuel cells.

The landlady, Ellie, seemed worried.

'If you've got far to go,' she said, 'it might be better to have a proper breakfast before you set off. You were very tired when you came in last night.'

And not much better now, she implied. That seemed to be the subtext.

He smiled and shook his head. 'Don't worry about me,' he said. 'I'm fine. I don't usually bother much with breakfast.'

She seemed about to argue, but instead, she smiled and turned to bring him the coffee and toast he had requested.

'I hope we'll see you again,' she said when he settled up prior to leaving.

'Anything's possible,' he told her.

Another smile. 'Safe journey,' she said.

He felt she meant it.

Afterwards, he got back on the road as quickly as he could and concentrated on the driving to the exclusion of everything else. There were people he could have called – emergency contact numbers, and so on – but he no longer trusted them, and couldn't bring himself to take the risk. He feared what they might say, and he doubted they would be concerned about his welfare anyway. Not now he had seen Jackson and Murphy at the scene.

More practically, a landline call would reveal his area code, and generally where he was, while a call from his mobile would allow them to pinpoint his location exactly. He didn't want that. He didn't want them to have any idea of his whereabouts, or his direction of travel either. When he did make contact, which he would do when it suited him, he would do it from an internet café.

He would have preferred them to be unaware that he was even back in the country, but there wasn't much he could do about that. He had to assume that routine passport monitoring at entry points would have told them that anyway. It would be stupid to hope that they might not have noticed, or that checks might have been suspended again because the Border Control Force still wasn't up to the job.

By 9.30 he had crossed the border just north of Berwick-upon-Tweed, and was pressing on into Scotland. Happily, the Scots still didn't require passport checks on entry. How much longer would that last, though, he wondered sourly.

He kept his speed down, not wanting a digital camera to record his passing. From now on, he reminded himself yet again, he had to be careful about every little thing.

In Edinburgh, he found an internet café and put out a message. I need help, he said to all the contact points. Something has gone wrong. Terrible things have happened.

Where are you? was what he got back. He sat and watched the replies come in. *Where are you?* Three of the four were quick. At the other station they must be having morning coffee, he decided. The thought wasn't amusing.

Where are you? It wasn't the response he had hoped for. *How can we help?* or *What do you need?* would have been better.

He closed down the connection and went to the counter to buy a coffee. Then he sat and watched George Street pass by. He sat at a little table towards the back, well away from the high seats in the window, but he wasn't comfortable. If anything, he felt even more vulnerable here, in a city. Anonymous, perhaps, but that also meant he didn't know who was observing him. It would be hard to see trouble coming.

And it would be. It would be coming. Trouble would have followed him home. It wouldn't have stopped at Calais. Not trouble like this.

Where are you? he thought again, bitterly. Fuck that!

So first they wanted to locate him. Why would they want to do that before asking what was wrong, discussing how they could help or assuring him of their unswerving support? Only one reason he could see; their priorities were higher than his personal safety. Probably, he was a nuisance, perhaps even a danger, to them. Foot soldiers like him didn't count for much. They never had done.

Moodily, he stirred his coffee. They were not like the other lot. The Russians brought their people home and looked after them: celebrated them; respected them. He had always known that. It made you wonder if you were on the right side.

Bastards!

'Have you finished with your cup?'

He looked up warily at the girl come to clear his table.

'What?'

'Your cup. Are you. . . ?'

He shook his head and pushed the cup towards her. She smiled and took it. He wondered what was wrong with her, smiling like that. Then he made an effort and smiled back.

'Thank you,' she said, before turning away.

He ought to practise that, he thought ruefully. Smiling at people. It might stand him in good stead. Not everybody was his enemy. Just the people who had always mattered most to him.

He would try them again, he decided. Maybe he'd been too hasty with his suspicions, and was being too cynical. Maybe – God forbid! – he was a touch paranoid.

But the answer was more or less the same. However he

phrased it, all they ever wanted to know was where he was.

For the last time, he typed with some frustration: I need help. Can you provide it? Back came the standard response:

We need to know where you are first.

Fuck that!

Angrily, he studied the messages, all four of them now. Coffee break must be over.

You could say that any offer of help would inevitably be constrained by consideration of his whereabouts. You could say that they really did need to know where he was before they could offer to do something. But his instincts said that was crap. They wanted to know where he was so they could send Jackson and Murphy after him, as well. Complete the tidying up. Leave no loose ends.

He frowned with thought. It was possible that he might be wrong – about every bloody thing! – but he was going to assume he was right. If he was wrong, nothing was spoilt. If he was right, then looking after himself his own way would give him – and Lisa – a better chance of surviving.

So he would go with his instincts. They had served him well so far.

Chapter Four

In Musselburgh he changed cars. He swapped the big Skoda that he was used to for an 8-year-old Land Rover Discovery, plus two thousand pounds that he paid in cash. Where he was headed next, he thought the 4-wheel drive would prove useful. He would have preferred a newer vehicle, but that would have required a bigger cash contribution, and he didn't want to flash too much of that about. As it was, the small-time dealer was happy to get his hands on a cash deal. He even knocked a bit off the price of the Land Rover in gratitude.

When he drove out of the yard he felt a bit better. If ever they caught onto the car he had been driving – perhaps through the ferry company – it wouldn't do them much good. He had broken the link.

He headed north, glad to put the city and its congestion behind him. The A9 took him up to Inverness that afternoon. Still he kept going, on into the darkness of early evening, on up the east coast until he could go no further. He had reached Thurso, and the adjacent harbour at Scrabster. It was too late to cross to Orkney, but he was well satisfied with his progress and content to settle down to spend a chilly night in the Land Rover.

The next morning, he was first in line to buy a ticket for the early ferry to Stromness. It was just as well because it took a little time, and the experience was worrying.

'I need to see your passport,' the woman in the ticket office said.

He was taken aback and stared at her for a moment. 'My passport?'

She nodded. 'Please.'

'For a journey inside the UK?'

'It's security regulations.'

It was hard to believe.

'I haven't got my passport with me,' he said desperately.

'Something official with your photo on it, then.'

He shook his head. The woman shrugged, and said she was sorry but there was nothing more she could do. They were required to be very security conscious these days.

He walked away. Outside, he stood grim-faced at a railing overlooking the harbour. Shit! Of all things. If he used his passport, it could give his whereabouts away to anyone looking for him. His trail would no longer be cold.

On the other hand, he decided eventually, this could also be a handy way of assessing the threat level.

Back in the office he handed over his passport.

'You found it?' the woman said.

He nodded. 'It was in the car, after all.'

Three hours later, he was on deck as the ship entered the harbour at Stromness. He felt good again, better anyway. Almost as far away from London as he could possibly get in the UK, he hoped to find sanctuary here, at least for a while.

But no sooner was he ashore than the doubts set in. His intention had been to head out to a small village, where once he had spent a little time on holiday. But now he felt he daren't leave Stromness. He had to stay, to see who came off the next couple of ferries.

There was all day to wait before the next ferry came in and by the time it did, the light wasn't very good. He stationed himself on a seat not far from the ramp that the vehicles used to leave the ship. They crawled past, giving him ample opportunity to see who was inside. There was no one who looked the part. None of the foot passengers or cyclists did either. You could never be sure, but he was pretty confident that nobody on this ferry had come after him.

He stayed where he was for another hour, in case of stragglers, but none came. That should have made him feel better, but it didn't. Not really. This was only one ferry. There would be plenty more.

He roused himself, got up, and found a B&B establishment not far away. For three nights, he said. Maybe more. He wasn't sure. The woman smiled and said they all said that, but they changed their minds when the magic of the islands got to work on them. Well, perhaps it would on him, too, he said.

The next morning, he was back at the quayside long before the ferry arrived. He stationed himself on the same seat, now wearing a fisherman's hat to shield his face from the bright sunlight, and identification.

He watched visitors inspecting the harbour, and the gulls inspecting them. Small boats left, some for a day's fishing, others for sightseeing or purposes unknown. Surprisingly, there were plenty of visitors, even at this time of year. Lots of English voices on all sides, too.

Orkney was like that, he knew, and very different from the Western Isles. No Gaelic spoken here, and altogether busier and more populated. Something to do with the modern oil industry, and a lot more to do with a different history featuring better farmland, Norse settlements and a railway all the way up the east coast of Scotland.

The hours passed. Eventually, he saw the ferry appear in the distance across Scapa Flow, and watched it steadily draw near and begin the big curving turn that would bring it safely into harbour. He adjusted his hat, straightening the peak to shadow his face, and sat still, waiting and watching.

They were in the third car to leave the ship: Jackson and Murphy. He winced, and ducked his head to study his newspaper as they passed without seeing him.

So they were here, he thought almost with satisfaction. His instincts had not let him down. The worst had come true. They were after him.

He left Mainland, the largest Orkney island, via the road across the Churchill Barriers, and took the Seacat from South Ronaldsway to Scotland. He landed near John o'Groats in the late afternoon and then headed south, leaving the Northern Isles to Jackson and Murphy. No way could he stay there now. They would find him if he did. Eventually they would. They were good at finding people who didn't want to be found.

The Land Rover was slow, too slow. Soon he regretted having it. Fine over rough country and local roads, but no good for getting anywhere fast. So back in Musselburgh that evening he changed vehicles again, trading in the Land Rover and another chunk of cash for a 3-year-old VW Passat.

'I'm not going to read in tomorrow's papers about a Land Rover having been used as a getaway vehicle in a bank robbery, am I?' the dealer asked with a chuckle.

'That was what I wanted it for,' he replied, 'but it didn't work out. That old tin can wouldn't do much more than 35.'

The dealer smiled. 'If you don't like this vehicle either,' he said, 'come back and see me again. Anytime. I'm always home to a good customer.'

He drove south, and then west, for a long time. In the small hours, he reached a place where he had kept a caravan for many years; more a retreat than a hideout, it was where he kept some personal stuff. Not valuable or confidential things, but clothes and equipment he needed when he headed into the mountains. Things he might need in an emergency, as well.

The caravan was on a long-stay site on a farm at the foot of Blencathra, midway between Penrith and Keswick, in the English Lake District. It wasn't an idyllic rose-covered cottage, this rural retreat, but he was attached to it. Lisa had liked it, too, which was another good reason to keep it.

He paid ground rent in advance, a year at a time, and rarely visited more than once a year. Sometimes not even that. But even in the years when he didn't come at all, he always knew it was there if he needed it. Given the way he lived, he needed somewhere like that. He felt he did, at least. And he needed it more than ever now, after the Prague disaster, and after Orkney hadn't worked out as he'd hoped.

He switched off the engine and lights when he was a couple of hundred yards away from the site and let the car roll slowly downhill on the track to the farm. He had no wish to wake anyone up in the middle of the night or to advertise his arrival. Someone would notice in the morning that he was here, but hopefully without much interest. Comings and goings were an everyday event, though more so in the summer months than this time of year. It was what helped to make it a good place for him to lay his head.

The gate leading on to the site was closed, as was usual at night; a security precaution. He gently slowed to a halt beside the farmhouse and got out to see if he could open the gate. A big padlock said no. That was a pity. But he wasn't seriously put out. The car could stop here for what remained of the night. That didn't mean he was denied the comfort of a bed. He could reach the caravan on foot, and get in using the key he kept taped to the underside.

He climbed over the gate and walked the twenty yards to the gap in the hawthorn hedge that sheltered the site from the worst of the winds. No tourers on site at this time of year but there were perhaps thirty static caravans, none with lights on just now. It wasn't a problem; starlight and a wispy moon let him see well enough. And what he saw brought him to a sudden halt.

He tensed and stood still. His eyes, and then his nose, confirmed it. Where his van should have been, there was an empty space. The acrid, smoky smell still hanging in the air told him what had happened to it. He stared with disbelief for a moment. Then he turned and started back to the car quickly, his heart pounding and his head swimming. They had beaten him to it. Somebody had.

Back on the road, he drove fast for a half hour. He headed south on the M6, instinct telling him he needed to put some miles on the clock. At the Tebay service area, he pulled off the motorway, stopped, and sat back to think. The caravan was gone. No use speculating about what had happened. His safe place couldn't have been safe after all, and now it no longer existed. They were closing him down. He swore bitterly.

The last vestige of doubt had been swept away. Orkney, and now this. They were after him, all right. God knew why.

He drummed his fingers on the steering wheel and thought about what to do next. He needed information. Badly. At the moment, he was running blind, knowing nothing. He couldn't go on like this.

There were people he could contact. One or two. Not officially, perhaps, but on a personal basis. Official channels would have to remain no-go areas for now.

First, though, there was something else he needed to check. He used the internet café in the service area to contact a storage depot in Slough. A 24/7 facility, it was where he kept another secret cache, this one of more personal stuff. Quickly, he gave the password and moved on through the pages to the one he wanted: the record of transactions.

He shook his head and stared at the screen with disbelief: empty. Gone. Every sodding thing taken out two days earlier – and not by him. Bastards! How had they known about this place?

He didn't bother even looking at his bank accounts. If they had got to his Slough storage bunker, they would certainly have got to his bank accounts and either closed them down or emptied them.

So now he had nothing left.

Almost nothing, he corrected himself. Just a car, a bag of money and a gun. Looking on the bright side, he thought grimly, you could do a lot with that.

He also had Lisa, of course. So, really, he had a lot more than nothing. He had everything that mattered. It was just that Lisa couldn't help. He had to keep her out of it.

Over an early breakfast, a thought came to him. Here he was on the edge of the Lake District, where Callerton – his old boss – lived somewhere in retirement. He even had a phone number for him on his mobile.

He switched on, which was a risk he had to take, and found the number. Then he switched back off and fed the number into one of the disposable phones he had picked up in Edinburgh. He glanced at his watch. Just after six. Too early? Fuck it! He'd wake the miserable old bastard up.

Chapter Five

The next lot of rain came sweeping across the land like a moving curtain, hiding everything in its path.

'Every fifteen fucking minutes,' Murphy said with disgust. 'It's worse than Ireland.'

Jackson buzzed the window closed and watched as the moving wall of grey-white enveloped the nearby farmhouse, then the barn next to it, and kept on coming until it felt like they were sitting beneath Niagara Falls.

'Ring him,' Murphy said suddenly.

'What? I can't hear you.'

'Ring him! Tell him.'

'Tell him what?' Jackson shrugged. There was no point trying to conduct a conversation until this lot moved on. No point phoning anybody either. He reached for a bottle of water.

Ten minutes later, things had calmed down. It was still raining heavily but the noisy downpour at the leading edge of this latest weather system had passed them by. He made the call.

'He's gone now,' Jackson was told. 'He left on the Seacat from South Ronaldsway.'

Jackson raised an eyebrow as he digested that bit of news. So they'd been wasting their time, sitting here like this?

'Get back onto the mainland. I've got somebody else doing things, but he's going to need help.'

'Doing things? What things?'

'We've been eliminating his bolt-holes and his bank accounts. He's running out of places to go and the things he needs to keep ahead of us.'

Jackson sighed. 'We'll probably have to stay overnight, and come back tomorrow. The ferries. . . .'

'I realize that. I'll let you know when we get another sighting report. And try to keep up next time!'

Jackson grimaced and switched off.

'What did he say?' Murphy asked.

Jackson told him. Murphy said, 'So we've been wasting our time?'

'We've made him move on. We must have been close. Anyway, he can't stay ahead for ever.'

Murphy said nothing for a moment. Then, 'You said that about the fucking rain. You said it couldn't rain forever!'

Jackson grinned. 'If only he'd been there in Prague, we wouldn't have had all this chasing to do. It would have been over and done with.'

'And we could have stayed there a bit longer. I liked Prague.'

'A bit cold, though. Remember?'

'Not all the time,' Murphy said, chuckling as he remembered. 'It got pretty warm in that flat when we turned up and they realized they'd come to the end of the road.'

'Yes,' Jackson agreed. 'It got pretty warm then. We did a neat and tidy job.'

'Apart from the one that got away.'

Jackson nodded and leaned forward to start the engine.

Chapter Six

The voice was tired and distant-sounding.

'Yes?'

No identifiers, he noted with a wry smile. Old habits.

'You told me to call you – anytime.'

He let that lie for a moment, time for it to sink in, his voice to be recognized.

'It's been a long time. How are you?'

A little interest had crept into the voice. That was encouraging.

'Troubled. I was wondering if it would be extremely inconvenient for me to visit you?'

Short pause; then:

'When? Today? Now?'

The voice was sharper now, sleep perhaps being pushed back, along with the covers.

'If possible. I'm not far away, you see.'

'And it's urgent, I assume?'

'Very.'

'You don't know where I live, do you?'

The voice was getting crisper by the minute.

'No.'

'Brackenrigg Cottage, Nether Wasdale.' Pause to glance at

watch or clock. 'Say about eleven?'

'Fine. See you then.'

He was about to add a pleasantry, but Callerton had switched off. Brief and to the point. Old habits again.

The timing of recent events was niggling away at him. So, soon after 7 a.m., he rang the farm, knowing the working day would be well underway by then. Mrs Ainslie, who together with her husband owned the place, answered.

'Oh, Mr Gibson! Terrible news, I'm afraid. I was wondering how we could contact you.'

'Mrs Ainslie?'

'The caravan – your caravan! It burned down. It's gone, I'm afraid. There's nothing left.'

He expressed astonishment.

'How did it happen, Mrs. Ainslie?'

'We don't know. We have no idea. We only wish we did. The fire service and the police have both been to investigate, and we're expecting them back again today. But they haven't said anything about what they've discovered.'

'Nobody hurt, I hope, Mrs Ainsley?'

'No, thank God! None of the caravans are occupied at the moment.'

'So there's been nobody there, on site?'

'No one at all, the past week or two. My husband thought he might have heard a car the other night, just after it got dark. And there seemed to be fresh tyre tracks in the morning, but we didn't see anyone. It's a bit scary, actually. We can't understand what's happened. And we're so very sorry, Mr Gibson.'

'It's not your fault. Don't you worry about that, Mrs Ainslie. So when did the . . . the fire happen, exactly?'

Just in time he had stopped himself saying 'attack' – when

had the attack happened?

'Wednesday night, early on. We heard an explosion, and then there were flames shooting into the sky. Whether it was a gas bottle. . . .'

'Probably.'

But unlikely, he thought grimly. Not the initial spark, anyway. Not the cause of it.

'Well, never mind, Mrs Ainslie. It was an old van and there was nothing of great value in it. I'll get the insurance company to contact you about a replacement. If that's all right with you?'

'Yes, of course it is. We're just so sorry this has happened, Mr Gibson.'

Not as sorry as I am, he noted grimly as he switched off. My best climbing boots were in that caravan.

Wednesday night then, he thought afterwards, drumming his fingers on the steering wheel. That was what he had wanted to establish. The bastards had certainly moved fast. Even before he was back in the country.

Firing the caravan had saved them time, as well as denying him the use of whatever he might have had in it. Searching it instead could have taken them hours, as well as making them visible.

He parked outside one of the two pubs in the tiny hamlet of Nether Wasdale. Then he took a stroll. It would be better to find Callerton's cottage himself, rather than leave someone with the memory of him asking where it was. By now, he had given up worrying that he might be being overly cautious. In his position, there was no such thing as too much caution.

He soon found the cottage. It was a few minutes' walk from the pub, down a lane that seemingly led nowhere very much. He smiled. Typical of Cally! Leaving London hadn't been enough. He had sought obscurity and isolation – and found them both.

It was a grand spot, he reflected, as he stood at the gate a moment and gazed around. Perfect; the fells, the lake, the ancient sycamores gnarled and twisted by wind and snow. Well deserved, too. Callerton had done his bit for Queen and Country, and then some.

He opened the gate and walked up the path towards the open front door. The old man would be ready for him. He always had been big on time keeping. Coffee would be ready, too, probably. Nothing alcoholic yet, though. Unless his habits had changed in retirement, that wouldn't happen until lunch was on the table.

He used the heavy door-knocker and eased the door further open, calling a greeting. There was no reply. Smiling, he paused, listening. Nothing. The silence continued. He called again, louder this time. Still nothing.

Alarm bells began to ring in his head. He frowned and stepped back. He brought out the Glock he had brought from Prague and checked it.

Cally wouldn't do this, he was thinking. The old man wouldn't fail to respond to a visitor's greeting. He wouldn't not be in either, not when an arrangement had been made and his visitor was exactly on time. He would be here, ready and waiting. Something was wrong.

He moved along the side of the house and looked through a window into what seemed to be the main living room. No one there. He moved on. Round the next corner was the kitchen window. He looked through it, winced and felt sick. He closed his eyes for a moment.

Callerton was there. He was slumped over the kitchen

table, immobile, in no position to receive visitors ever again.

The back of his head was a mess. Even from the window he could see that. A bullet, almost certainly, and whoever had fired it had been standing right behind him.

So they'd got here before him. Christ, they'd been quick off the mark – again!

It couldn't have been Jackson and Murphy, though. They hadn't had time to get off Orkney and down here, even if they had known this was where he was coming. Someone else, then. Another team. Or just one man. Less suspicious. The arrival of a team might have alerted Callerton.

The question was, where was the gunman now? Here still? If not, then not long gone. There hadn't been time. Quite possibly still around, waiting for him to arrive.

He glanced back round the corner of the cottage. No one had appeared to seal off his exit route. He hesitated, weighing up his options. They were limited and straightforward: either he left immediately or he took a look inside first.

He thought quickly. There was just a faint chance the old man might have prepared something that might help. So he'd better chance it, and look inside before he left.

He wiped his face with his sleeve and checked the gun again. Then he headed back to the front door and stepped into the front porch, calling out as if he was unaware anything was wrong.

The cottage was small. Two storeys, with probably only two rooms upstairs. The gunman, if he hadn't already departed, wouldn't be upstairs. The priority spaces were all down below. The living room. The kitchen. What else was there? Probably a scullery. Possibly a separate dining room, but it would be a small one.

'Cally?'

He called again and rattled about a bit in the porch. Then he laid down on the floor and eased his head around the living room door. Nothing. No one. He slid slowly into the room on his belly, and lay still.

As well as cupboards, a dresser, and free-standing bookshelves, there was an old, upright-style, three-piece suite on wooden legs. From his position on the floor, he could see the legs of a man kneeling behind the settee. The gunman had not left.

He pushed the door hard, forcing it back to crash against the wall. A man leapt up from behind the settee, arms braced to fire the gun he was holding.

There was no time, no time for anything at all. The air filled with dust, as bullets hit the wall and the door, where he should have been standing. Harry fired, and kept on firing until the gun pointing at him flew through the air, and the man who had been holding it slumped to the floor.

He scrambled across the room, ears ringing, pulse racing, and kicked the dropped gun aside. Then he stooped and felt for a pulse: there wasn't one.

He straightened up and took a few moments to recover and let his pulse rate begin to drop back down. He wriggled his shoulders and stretched, working some of the tension out of his body. Then he leaned down again to see what he had shot.

The man was a stranger to him. Perhaps 30-ish, short-haired and tidy-looking. He wore jeans and a casual outdoor jacket. There was nothing in his pockets to say who or what he was; only car keys and spare ammunition. All in all, that was a pretty good indication of who or what he was. Leave no trace. That was a cardinal rule for the cleaners.

A minute or two had elapsed by then, and no one else had appeared. He stood up and went quickly though the cottage, room by room, satisfying himself that no one else was in the building. It seemed to have been a one-man operation, as he had guessed. Not top notch either. They had just sent whoever was available and could get here in time.

But why? What the hell was it about? This seemed even more senseless than the killings in Prague. Cally was not a player, not any more. He'd been out of it for several years. He shook his head, feeling utterly depressed. He had liked the old man. Respected him, as well. His murder now was so pointless.

Pulling himself together, he took stock of what he knew and could see. Cally must have accepted his killer's credentials. He would never have let the man inside the cottage otherwise.

Perhaps consultations with people from the department had still happened from time to time? It wasn't impossible. Cally was – had been – a living archive. They might well have needed to consult him occasionally.

He returned to the kitchen and studied the scene there. Callerton was seated at the table. It looked as though he had been going through his morning's paper, *The Times*, when the bullet had arrived. He had been waiting; waiting for his eleven o'clock visitor.

He glanced at the open page, grimaced and shook his head. Pen in hand, Cally had been reading an article on Siberian gas fields in the business section. He had even circled the subheading. Keeping an eye on his investments?

A last glance around. Then he turned and made his way outside and headed back towards the car. There was nothing here for him now. Nothing at all. Perhaps there wouldn't have been anyway. It was doubtful if Cally had still been in the loop.

But in that case why had he been murdered?

And surely it was no coincidence that the shooting had happened shortly before he himself had been due to arrive to talk to him? No, of course it bloody wasn't! They must have known he was coming. They would have been monitoring the phone.

Not his phone, though. Cally's. He himself had used a cheap, disposable phone, and got rid of it as soon as the call was finished. It would have been Cally's that they had been monitoring.

They had probably guessed he might try to contact the old man. Once he had actually done that, they must have decided it was an opportunity to get rid of them both; himself and Cally.

But he couldn't even begin to guess as to why. No idea at all.

He shook his head. What was more, try as he might, he couldn't get one step ahead of them. So far, they had anticipated his every move. They were boxing him in.

At least they still didn't know about Lisa. He faltered. They didn't, did they? Surely not?

He realized then that he had no idea. He shivered and suddenly felt very cold. Until now, he had assumed that if he kept away from Lisa, and didn't contact her, she would be safe. Now he just didn't know any more. It was terrifying.

Chapter Seven

He headed back to Northumberland on automatic pilot. There was nowhere else he could think of going. He returned to The Running Man, a place with which he had no known connection, and where nobody knew him. The one night he had spent there lingered in his memory now as a time of peace and tranquillity.

They seemed glad to see him again, especially Ellie.

'We don't get a lot of visitors at this time of year,' she admitted. 'So you can have the same room, if you like.'

He took it.

'Mr Gibson, isn't it?'

He nodded and smiled. That would do for now. His passport, the one he was using at present, said different, but by now he could scarcely recall the name he'd started out with. What was in a name, anyway?

But he kept 'Harry'. That would always be with him. You had to have something to cling to.

'It's Harry,' he volunteered.

She nodded, as if that explained a lot.

'Harry,' she repeated.

The night was a difficult one. He didn't feel under immediate threat, not here, but his head was in turmoil. He knew now for sure that he was deep in trouble. There was no longer any possibility of it all being a mistake, or of him being an innocent bystander. He was in the middle of it, even if he had no idea why. He was alone too, more alone than he had ever been.

There had been four of them in Unit 89, the special unit Callerton had set up after the Soviet withdrawal from Central Europe. He was now the only one left, and if they got him as well, it would be as if Unit 89 had never existed. He doubted there would even be a paper trail for future historians to follow; there would be nothing, nothing at all.

And he really was out on a limb. No personal contact with London any more, not since Callerton had retired. Callerton's immediate successor had soon moved on, and now he didn't even know the name of the man who had taken his place. All his reports went via cut-outs, when they didn't simply go by post or electronic transmission. Landis had been the only one with direct, face-to-face contact. And now he had a hole in the back of his head, like the other members of Unit 89.

The elimination of the unit? Harry blinked with surprise as the thought registered. Was that what this was about? The elimination of Unit 89? Could that be the explanation?

Surely not? It was an absurd notion, but no more so than what had been happening these past several days. Whoever would have thought any of it possible?

His attempts to make sense of it all won him a sleepless night. It was dawn when finally he got to sleep, and then he missed breakfast and had to settle for lunch instead.

'It's no problem,' Ellie said when finally he made his way downstairs. 'Nothing's spoiling, and you needed some sleep.'

She gave him a happy smile and added, 'Order what you

like. The chef is longing to cook something for somebody. So what's it going to be – bacon and eggs, or steak and chips?'

He settled for the lamb stew that topped the lunch menu that day.

'You're very easy-going here,' he added.

'I'm afraid we are. Some might think it a fault, but I don't suppose we'll ever change.'

He laughed. 'The whole village is like that, is it?'

'It is. I don't think you would like it at all.'

'Oh?'

'Well, you obviously lead a very busy life, rushing here, there and everywhere – and never getting enough sleep!'

'It's been like that lately,' he admitted, 'but it's not what I would choose. Easy-going would suit me very well indeed.'

'Would it really?' she asked mischievously before sweeping away to see to new customers in the dining room.

Really, he thought wearily. In another life.

Afterwards, he took a stroll around the village. In other circumstances, he thought again, he could have been happy with what he saw here; the village green, the river, the ancient, gnarled trees, and the little school where he could hear children playing in the yard during their lunch break. He was out of touch these days with metropolitan England, but this England he could relate to very easily. At least, he would have been able to if his head hadn't been full of questions, and pictures of dead bodies.

He spent a little time thinking about Jackson and Murphy. So far as he could see, there was no way they could find him here. Not unless he made a mistake and unwittingly brought them to his door. To all intents and purposes, he was off the map so long as he remained here and contacted nobody.

He toyed with the idea of staying, and finding somewhere in the village to live. Fantasy, perhaps, but it had its attractions. He could do it. Live here. Maybe even bring Lisa, in time. Then, when the money ran out, he could get a little job. Deliver mail, or help look after sheep. There was bound to be something he could do. Work in the local abattoir, he thought sourly. He'd be good at that.

An estate agent's window caught and held his attention for a few minutes. There were places to rent as well as to buy, and often at prices that didn't seem absurd. One, in particular, caught his eye: Bracken Cottage, with three bedrooms, a mile outside the village centre. Roses at the door? he wondered with a smile.

But perhaps he would be better off with somewhere actually in the village; a cottage or a flat with more immediate access to whatever services were available here. The pub notably, he thought with another smile. Oh, well. One day, perhaps. It was something to dream about.

The trouble was, staying here wouldn't answer any of his questions. There were no answers in this village, pleasant and safe as it was, and he wasn't ready to settle for that. He needed to know what was going on. He needed to see Lisa, as well, but that would have to wait a while. It was too risky and dangerous. Forget that, for now.

Back at the hotel, he picked up another of his disposable phones and began to punch in the numbers. Once he got started, he found he could remember the sequence easily. But there was no reply when he pressed send. He frowned, put down the phone and had another think. Then he began to pack. It was time to go.

'You're not leaving already?' Ellie said, visibly disappointed.

'I'm afraid so.'

'That's a pity. It was so nice to have a guest,' she said with a chuckle. 'It makes a change for us all.'

He smiled. 'I'd like to come back,' he said.

'Please do.'

'I might look at some of the properties in the estate agent's window,' he added, wanting to extend the conversation.

'Oh?' She looked searchingly at him, not smiling now. 'You really do like it here, don't you?'

'Yes, I do.' He stared back at her, knowing then that something was going on between them. 'I'd like to see you again, Ellie, as well. You'll still be here?'

She nodded. 'I'll be here. I have to be. It's my hotel.'

Then she leant forward and brushed his cheek with her lips.

'Take care,' she said, looking worried now, and for all the world as if she understood the signs and realized he had an uncertain future, ringed by danger.

He crossed the Channel from Dover to Dunkirk that night, and didn't care if they discovered he had left the country again. Hopefully, it would just seem that he had left because inside its borders he had not found the safe haven he had sought. They would have no idea where he was bound.

Back in Prague, he kept well away from Vyšehrad. He had no intention of going anywhere near the safe house or the flat where he had lived in recent months. He didn't believe in tempting fate.

The first night he booked into a pension just off Karlovo Náměstí – Charles Square – in the university area. He felt he ought to be safe enough there for one night. But he still took the gun to bed with him. Somewhere, back there, Jackson and Murphy would be on his trail. And if not them, then others. He was a marked man.

The room was small and overheated. He opened the window and listened to the night sounds: the crowds and the trams, the traffic, and somewhere the sound of a traditional jazz band playing joyously. It felt surprisingly good to be back, back in this city he knew so well. Familiarity was a great comfort. For a time, it took away thoughts of what had happened here, and of what he had to do.

He dozed for an hour or so. After midnight, the crowds dispersed, the traffic stopped and most of the trams went home for a few hours, leaving only the hourly night service to rumble between the buildings. Then, at last, he could sleep properly.

In the morning, he ate breakfast in a nearby café, choosing sliced cheese and salami to go with the traditional Turkish-style coffee that came in the equally traditional glass mug without handles. Afterwards, he took a tram out to Strašnická.

It was a dismal journey, out beyond the areas tourists never reached, past the old, run-down blocks of flats and the dilapidated industrial premises, and into the zone of shabby blocks of workers' flats built in the 1960s and 70s. Beautiful Prague it was not. Strašnická was an area, one of many in the outlying districts, that didn't feature in the guide books and the celebratory videos. It was as bad, he reflected, as the train journey through north London.

His fellow passengers didn't include anyone who looked like a potential assassin. No Jackson or Murphy types, not that appearances counted for much in that regard. Still. . . . He stayed alert, vigilant.

Mostly, the others in his tram were either young women with infants or elderly people, the latter often infirm of mind or body, and sometimes both. Everyone else would be at work. He eyed and almost welcomed the bearded, smelly tramp who planted himself in a nearby seat. Definitely not department material, he thought with an inner smile.

Once a separate place in its own right, Strašnická had a New Town and an Old Town. He left the tram in the Old Town, a busy shopping area with a department store and plenty of little cafés and family-owned shops. It was a working-class, industrial area, very definitely. And he felt better here, better than since the trouble had started. He was back in the world he had long inhabited, and the familiarity of it was like a tonic. Here, he could drift invisibly, and with the growing confidence that came with anonymity.

He made his way out of the shopping precinct and walked steadily past several large blocks of flats. He knew where he was going. He only hoped this little bit of the world hadn't changed since his last visit.

Kosmonauto 68. He was here. This was it, the address. He walked up to the entrance to the ten-storey block of flats and studied the names of the tenants alongside the buttons for the buzzers on their individual front doors.

There it was! She was still here. His finger moved to the button alongside the name: Novotná.

Chapter Eight

'Just get back to Prague.'

Jackson pulled the phone away from his ear for a moment and glanced at it with disbelief.

'Are you sure?' he asked.

'I hope you're not questioning my orders?'

'No, of course not.' He caught Murphy's eye and shrugged dramatically.

'Gibson has left the country again. We don't know where he is but my guess is he'll end up back in Prague. So that's where I want you.'

'Fair enough.'

Afterwards, Murphy said, 'What now?'

'He wants us back in Prague. He says that's where Gibson will eventually end up.'

'So he's left the UK?'

'Apparently.'

Murphy grumbled on a bit about all the extra driving. Jackson let him. He was thinking about Gibson, trying to see the world through his eyes. What would he do? Where would he go?

'It's obvious,' Jackson announced with some satisfaction. 'The boss is right. Gibson has to return to Prague. That's the only place where he knows people. He's been out in the field too long. We've seen it before, haven't we?'

Murphy nodded. 'They used to call it bush happy – going native. In the old days.'

Jackson agreed. 'They aren't happy anywhere else. It gets to them in the end.'

'Then we get to them,' Murphy said with satisfaction.

'What would they do without us?'

'They'd struggle.'

And that was the truth of it, Jackson thought. The department would be unable to cope with its awkward ex-employees. It would be on its knees with accumulated lawsuits and enquiries, its operational budget draining away into the sand.

'Remember that one we followed to Patagonia?' Murphy said.

'The ends of the earth!' Jackson grinned. 'Thought he'd got away, didn't he?'

'They always do. This one will be the same.'

'They don't get away from us, though,' Jackson said. 'They never do.'

Murphy nodded agreement.

They were a good team, Jackson reflected. The best. Even the Russians wouldn't have anybody better than them.

'The thing is,' Murphy said, equally reflectively, 'in our line of work, you have to be an enthusiast. You have to like it. The hunt, the kill, everything.'

Now it was Jackson's turn to nod agreement. That was the truth of it. You had to like it, enjoy doing it, and they did. They had proved that over and over again. Sometimes he wondered if maybe Murphy didn't enjoy it too much, but. . . . What the hell!

'Which airport do you want to go from?' he asked.

Murphy chuckled. 'Am I glad to hear you ask that! I'm sick of this damned car.'

'So which one?'

'Any one but Heathrow.'

Chapter Nine

He hesitated. He was anxious to get on, but rushing into it might be a mistake.

For a start, he didn't know if she really was here still. Her name was, but she might have moved out and sublet the flat. It was a common enough thing to do. The right to occupy a flat, whether owned or rented, had always been invaluable. People hung on to that right when they had it.

Even if she was living here still, he had no idea who else might be with her. And how eager would she be to see him anyway? His finger fell away from the button. He turned and walked off. He would wait. It was safer.

There was a small children's play area fifty yards from the entrance to the flats. Next to it was a picnic table with a couple of benches. He tried sitting there but he felt too conspicuous. He got up and walked around for a while, always keeping sight of the entrance to the block of flats where she used to live, and perhaps did still.

There was nothing special about the building, not on the outside. It was simply one of many such blocks of flats alongside the main road and the tram tracks, in long lines stretching away into the distance. The flats would have been prized new housing when they were built, and not only for manual workers either. It hadn't been like that here. People had been all in it together under socialism; road sweepers and headteachers, factory managers and bus drivers, all living side by side. Sometimes in heavenly peace, sometimes in a makeshift Bronx. It had all depended on your neighbours.

He was nervous, anxious. Had he got it right? Could he trust her? Was she even here still? The questions went round and round in his head. If the answer to any of them was no, he would have to think of something else.

She came out in a rush at 7.45 in a well-rehearsed start to her day, a particular tram in mind. So she was still here, he thought with relief.

He caught up with her halfway to the tram stop, coming in at an angle, knowing she would be aware of his approach even though she hadn't turned her head to glance in his direction. He fell in behind. He didn't want to startle her.

'Don't stop, Lenka!' he urged in Czech. 'Don't look round. Keep going. But I need to see you.'

However startled she was by his arrival, her pace never faltered and she didn't look round. She kept going, a couple of paces ahead of him. It would have been surprising if an observer had detected any communication between them.

The tram stop was in the middle of the road, a long, thin, unguarded strip of raised pavement, with traffic passing dangerously close by on both sides. They crossed two traffic lanes to reach it and then separated, mingling with a dozen other people also waiting, in a sprawl rather than a formal queue.

He studied the empty spaces between blocks of flats on the other side of the road. Others stared along the tracks, willing the tram to appear round the distant corner. The waiting game. It was up to her now. He had made contact. She would decide how she wanted to play it, if indeed she wanted to play at all.

She would have been surprised, astonished probably, by his approach, but she didn't know how toxic he was. In the circumstances, she had responded well. She had followed his lead. He had given her time to think, and now he awaited her response.

When she left the tram, he stayed where he was and watched her head across the street and enter a small café on the far side. He stayed on the tram as far as the next stop. He got off there and waited to see who else did. No one at all. He walked back at a brisk pace, sure that no one had followed him.

The café was small and busy. A lot of the trade was from people passing through to pick up a coffee to take with them. He joined her at a small table tucked away in a corner.

'Mr Gibson!' she murmured in English with a small smile. 'Such a delightful surprise. How are you, Harry?'

'Hello, Lenka.' He smiled back ruefully. 'I'm all right – so far. Thanks for agreeing to meet.'

She shrugged.

He sat down. 'Coffee?'

'I've already ordered – for both of us.'

'As efficient as ever!'

She laughed and took out a cigarette packet. He shook his head when she offered it to him and waited while she lit a cigarette for herself.

'I'm in trouble, Lenka,' he said then. 'I'm hoping you might know, or be able to find out, what's going on.'

She gazed out across the café, lifted her head slightly and

blew a stream of smoke towards the ceiling.

'How bad is it, this trouble, on a scale of one to ten?'

'Ten.'

She sighed and shook her head. 'Then it's not me you need to see, Harry. I'm not the one to give help on that scale.'

A waitress came near, collecting dirty cups and plates. Then another one arrived with their coffee. Nothing more was said while they were in earshot.

'So what is the problem?' Lenka asked when both waitresses had moved away.

'You know what I do?'

She nodded. 'Of course. Like us, you keep an eye on the Russians.'

'Yes, the bloody Russians!' he said with a sigh and a shake of the head. 'How many of their agents are here in Prague these days?'

'At the last count?'

'To the nearest thousand,' he said with a smile.

She chuckled. 'They have been reluctant to let my country go. I think they have more agents here now than ever.' She shrugged. 'Maybe they just like it here.'

He watched her draw on her cigarette and waited for her to cough, remembering how it used to be for him in the mornings when he was a smoker.

She cleared her throat and stubbed out the half-smoked cigarette.

'I should give up,' she said ruefully, rubbing one eye with the back of her hand.

He kept his thoughts on that subject to himself.

'Parliament was shocked the other year,' she said, 'when for the first time the minister described the situation with Russian agents in his annual report on the security service.

He admitted there were more now than ever.'

'I remember. We thought then that something might be done about it, once it was out in the open. But it wasn't, was it?'

She shook her head. 'What could we do? We just live with it – and with them. They're everywhere. As with you, in London. Maybe it's better this way, better than how it used to be. I don't know.'

Maybe it was. He didn't know either. This had always been a country where the intelligence services watched each other, and made contact and arranged deals when necessary. It wasn't neutral territory, like Austria. More of a common stomping ground. But that wasn't his concern right now.

'My unit has been wiped out,' he said, leaning forward.

Her brow wrinkled in a query.

'Unit 89, as it was called – after the big convulsions in this part of the world. Eliminated. I'm the only survivor, and I don't know how long that will last.'

She stared at him. 'What do you mean, Harry?'

He told her. Everything. He told her about the safe house, the regular meetings, the care they took, and the massacre he had discovered a few days ago.

'It's worse than you might think,' he added wearily. 'The Russians didn't do the killing.'

She listened with a grim face as he told her what he had observed and about the efforts made to hunt him down since then.

'It is incredible,' she said when he was finished.

'Isn't it?' He shook his head and added bitterly, 'It took me a while to get used to it.'

'But you came back here?'

'Here is where it started. Here is where I've been for many

years. The explanation has to be here, somewhere. That's what I was hoping you might be able to help me with.'

She shook her head. 'I know nothing about any of this, Harry. I don't even know if the bodies of your colleagues have been found yet.'

He gave her the address of the safe house, but warned that the bodies might have been removed in a clear-up operation.

'What were you working on?' she asked. 'At the time, I mean. Anything special?'

He shook his head. 'I certainly wasn't. Routine stuff, basically. Tracking. Keeping an eye on the agents we knew about. The usual.'

'Nothing out of the ordinary? No warning signs?'

'Nothing. To be honest, I've been wondering for some time why we bother any more. It's all so routine. It might have been important in the past, but these days. . . .' He stopped and shrugged. 'I was hoping you. . . .'

'I'll see what I can find out.' She glanced at her watch. 'But now I must go. I have a meeting to attend.'

'Of course.'

'Where are you staying?'

'I'm moving around. I don't feel I can afford to stay anywhere for long.'

She reached into her bag, took out a pen and scribbled an address on a piece of paper. 'Stay there,' she said. 'It is safe.'

'Officially safe?' he asked dubiously.

'No, not that. It is a building owned by a friend. Give him my name, and ask for accommodation. I will come this evening.'

He nodded. 'Thanks.'

She pushed her chair back and stood up. 'Take care, Harry,' she said, leaning forward to peck him on the cheek.

He stayed where he was, watching her through the window until she boarded a tram that would take her into the city centre. She knew nothing, apparently. He wondered why he had thought she might. And he wondered again if he could trust her. Probably not, he decided with regret. He couldn't afford to trust anyone.

Chapter Ten

He found his way to the address Lenka had given him. It was in Malá Strana – The Little Quarter – on the west bank of the river and close to the city centre. He got off the tram at Divadlo Národní, the National Theatre, and walked over Charles Bridge, easing his way through the visiting hordes of tourists, increasing numbers of whom were Russians these days. Sign of the times, he thought. The Russians were everywhere now they had money, and they especially liked it here. At least they didn't come in tanks these days.

The street he sought was a narrow canyon between nineteenth-century apartment buildings that fronted directly onto the pavement. Dark and quiet, it sheltered a thousand people, perhaps more, behind its sandstone walls. He felt conspicuous, possibly watched, as he walked alone along the street, mindful of the quiet. He grew uneasy, and almost sorry to have left Charles Bridge and its teeming, noisy visitors behind.

He walked past the address he had been given, carrying on without pause to the end of the street. Then he turned, stepped into a doorway and waited a few moments before setting off to retrace his footsteps. There was still no one in sight. It felt too quiet, but what could you do? Nothing. He walked the full length of the street again and then headed over towards the river. He had seen enough.

The ground floor of the building he wanted was occupied by a small restaurant called Jana, a combination bar and café. The menu board outside suggested it was not aimed at tourists. The meals on offer were simple and traditional, and a tenth of the price they would have been just a couple of blocks away on the tourist trail up Mostecká towards the cathedral and the castle. The name he had been given was presumably the name of the proprietor: Jan Klaus.

He would come back later, he decided. There was no reason to spend longer here, or in any other place, than necessary. Movement suited him better. What he needed was not a bed, or even a meal: it was information. And for that, he was pinning his hopes on Lenka.

It was a long day, a day spent unobtrusively in the shadows at the edge of a busy, noisy world. He fretted, inevitably, but he steeled himself to wait and see what Lenka came up with. If it was nothing, which he half-expected, he would have to move on and think again. Meanwhile, he tried not to think about Lisa. That was hard too, but necessary.

He moved the car across the river, parking it on a quiet street a couple of blocks away from Jan Klaus's establishment. Then he whiled away the hours on a small island, a little way upstream from Charles Bridge, where there were wandering visitors, but not too many. From where he sat beneath a lime tree, he could see what was happening all across the island, and felt reasonably safe.

Leaves drifted down gently from the great trees all around him and the scent of autumn was heavy on the air. But the sun was warm still, despite the month, and in other circumstances it would have been a Prague day to enjoy. As it was, his mind was racing too fast, constantly retracing recent events, trying to make sense of them but getting nowhere.

Lisa was never far from his thoughts and eventually he gave up the attempt to put her out of his mind. At some point soon, he would have to find a way of checking on her. Not yet, though. He couldn't risk exposing her to the dangers besetting him. As far as he knew, Lisa was safe. He wanted to keep her that way.

The afternoon wore on slowly but eventually the sun did begin to sink, and with it the temperature. It was almost a relief. A little before 4 p.m., he stood up and set off back towards the address Lenka had given him, trudging through the fallen leaves covering the grass. For a moment, he wondered if it would be like this in Northumberland too, but it required a greater feat of imagination than he was capable of at that moment. He let the thought go.

Jan Klaus's street was quiet still. There were no suspicious parked cars or loitering pedestrians. He stepped into a doorway and waited there for a couple of minutes. Briefly, playing devil's advocate, he considered again the possibility that Lenka might not be on his side, after all. He soon dismissed that possibility. If he couldn't count on Lenka, he might as well give up and surrender – or just shoot himself now, and get it over with. He emerged from the doorway and headed for the restaurant along the street.

There were half a dozen customers in place. He could see them all as soon as he entered the restaurant. Jana was small, no more than a single, L-shaped room plus a hidden kitchen. Beer drinkers sat at tables close to the bar in the short L-part of the room, one group playing a game of cards, others watching the television mounted on the wall in a desultory, late-afternoon sort of way. In the larger dining area, there were a dozen tables, two of them occupied by young couples eating meals. He sat at a vacant table near a window.

A waitress, a young girl, appeared very quickly. He ordered *pivo,* beer, *brambory polévka,* potato soup and *guláš.* He also asked if Jan Klaus was around. The girl scribbled his order on a notepad and said she would check about the other.

The *pivo* arrived very quickly, as normal. He smiled his gratitude. *Pivo* always received urgent attention in traditional Czech restaurants. It was part of the culture, a culture he appreciated, and in which he was at home after so long spent here.

How long, exactly? he asked himself. He couldn't remember, not exactly. Quite a few years, though. It had all started with occasional visits, which had then become frequent visits. Finally, Cally had suggested he just stay here. That was after he had set up Unit 89. The ostensible reason was to save travel costs, but he had known the proposal was an accolade, and that in effect it meant the old man was appreciative of his work and trusted him.

He shrugged. All that was in the past. To hell with it! His priorities now were Lisa and himself. Everything else was nothing to do with him any more. He was finished with it all.

'Can I help you?'

He looked up at the large, round man who had quietly appeared alongside his table. The man had come through a discreet door at the back of the dining room. Probably a doorway to the kitchen.

'Pán Klaus?'

The man nodded.

'Novotná sent me. She suggested you might be able to provide me with temporary accommodation.'

Klaus studied him for a moment, as if awaiting proof of his credentials.

'Lenka herself will come this evening,' he added. 'She is an old friend.'

'And colleague?'

He nodded. 'Something like that.'

Klaus glanced round. There was no one in earshot.

'Perhaps there is some difficulty?' he suggested.

'Perhaps.'

Klaus nodded with apparent satisfaction. 'Eat,' he suggested. 'Eat, and afterwards I will take you to your room.'

'Thank you.'

The man nodded and left.

The room was simple, clean and perfectly adequate. It comprised. . . . Enough! No point making an inventory, he decided. He wasn't going to live here.

Once he had decided the room was satisfactory, he left to bring his bags from the car. Then he settled down to wait.

A slight breeze from the open window tickled the curtain. A motorbike roared along the street. Distant voices told him tourists still thronged Charles Bridge. But this building itself was still and quiet. He could hear his watch measuring out time.

Just before 7 p.m., his ears detected creaks in the corridor outside his room. He stood up, tensed.

Fingernails tapped lightly on his door.

'Yes?' he said quietly.

'I am here.'

Lenka. With relief, he opened the door and let her inside.

Before he closed the door again, he glanced automatically both ways along the corridor. There was no one else. He turned to face her with a welcoming smile.

'It is not good,' she said with a weary shrug. 'It is not good at all.'

Chapter Eleven

He steered her to a chair and sat down himself.

'Tell me,' he said.

She stared bleakly at him.

'Whatever you have heard,' he said gently, 'I've done nothing you don't know about, and nothing you would regard as wrong. As far as I know, that was true of my colleagues, as well.'

He shook his head with exasperation. 'I haven't a clue as to what's been going on.'

Lenka yawned, stretched and leaned forward.

'Harry, my ministry doesn't know what is going on either. We are not in the loop. So what I tell you now is more best guess than fact. OK?'

He nodded.

She sighed and said bluntly, 'We believe your people have done a deal with the Russians. Part of the price was the elimination of your Unit 89.'

He stared at her with astonishment. 'And that's it? That's what you've come up with?'

She nodded. 'Our best guess.'

'Crap!' he said angrily. 'Absolute bloody rubbish! They would never do that.'

'Not even if the rewards were very high?'

'Of course not!'

He got up and began to pace around the room. What he'd just said was wrong. He knew that as soon as he'd said it. He had seen the cleaners at the safe house. They had followed him to Orkney, for God's sake! Not to mention what they'd done to Cally – and his bloody caravan!

She could be right.

He leaned against a blank wall. He pressed his face against the cool whiteness and let some of the heat drain out of his face.

'Harry?'

He straightened up and turned around reluctantly. He stared at her and shook his head, more in despair than denial now.

'This is what we believe,' Lenka said quietly.

'What could the UK possibly want from Russia that badly?'

She shook her head. 'We have no idea. But surely there are many things your country might want? Better relations, for example. Or the return of important prisoners. The release of human rights organizers? I don't know.'

He shook his head. 'Nothing like that. It would have to be something urgent and really important. National security, perhaps. Even then. . . .'

He spun away for a moment and then turned back to her again.

'It's difficult for me to see this with your objectivity.'

She nodded. 'I understand. Perhaps it is not true anyway. It is just our. . . .'

'I know. Your best guess.'

She gave a little shrug and looked away, and he wondered

if she was holding something back.

'What?' he pressed. 'What else?'

She turned back to him, her expression blank.

'There's something else, isn't there?'

She nodded. 'There is, yes. Sit down, Harry – please.'

Reluctantly, he sat down.

With another little shrug, almost an apology, she said, 'You have a child, Harry.'

His heart began to race. He struggled to keep his own face blank now. 'A child?' he said.

She nodded. 'You and Marika had a baby girl. The child will now be six, or perhaps seven.'

'Whatever makes you say that?' he said with a hoarse chuckle.

'It is on file. Perhaps the file is wrong?'

He said nothing. How did she know? How did *they* know? Even more important, if they knew, who else knew?

'I believe the file is correct,' Lenka said matter-of-factly.

Still he said nothing.

'Perhaps it is not my business,' Lenka added, getting up. 'But I must warn you that we believe the child is in danger.'

He got up, too, anguish tearing him apart.

'No, Harry. You don't need to say anything now. But think about it. I will return later.'

She delved into her pocket and produced a slip of card, on which she quickly wrote something. 'Use this number to contact me. It is safe. And you are safe here – for the moment.'

He took it and nodded. 'Thank you, Lenka.'

'Remember,' she said, 'that Marika was my friend.'

Afterwards, he wondered what on earth was going on, and what, if anything, he could do about it. Could Lenka possibly be right about a deal having been struck? She knew about Lisa, after all. Could she be right about HMG doing a deal with the Russians, as well?

It was possible. He knew that. The killings, and the way he had been pursued, hadn't left him with many illusions. Somebody was intent on ridding the world of Unit 89.

But Lisa? He frowned. Why would she be in danger?

It was so frustrating. Worse. He had done everything he could to keep Lisa safe. Since the moment she was born, he had always had her safety in mind. He had promised Marika that, and Marika's death had made him even more careful. Lisa's very existence had been kept secret. Or so he had thought, until now. What had changed?

When Lenka returned he would have to press her, even though that would mean admitting that he did indeed have a child. Continued denial was no longer a viable option.

Jesus Christ! She knew already. He'd better get real. If Lenka knew, then others knew. Her whole bloody ministry, for a start! And who else besides?

At least they didn't know where Lisa was.

He thought again. Did they? Sickened, he realized he could no longer be sure, either about that or anything else. His whole world had been turned upside down.

There wasn't much he could do before Lenka returned. But there was one thing: the room had a phone, and he used it. The time had come.

'Paní Čechová?'

'Mr Harry!'

'Hello, Babička! Grandmother! How are you? And how is Lisa?'

'We are well, thank you. Everything is normal here. Lisa

often asks for you. More and more, she asks for you. Excuse me. I will get her now.'

'No! Not yet, Babi. One moment, please.'

He closed his eyes with relief. Lisa was well. Nothing had happened.

'Babička, thank you so much for everything you have done for Lisa. I am so grateful. Marika would be, too. You have been wonderful.'

'Lisa is my grandchild,' the old woman said simply.

'I know, I know, but still. . . . Babi, has anything unusual happened recently?'

'I don't think so,' she said, sounding puzzled. 'No, nothing.'

'That's good. I don't want to worry you, but please take care. Now I will speak to Lisa.'

Nothing, he thought with relief, while he waited for Babička to bring his child to the phone. Good so far. But for how much longer?

'Father!'

'Lisa!' He smiled and chuckled. 'How are you, my dear?'

'My English language is very good now, I think.'

It all came out in a rush, as if she knew there would not be much time, as usual.

'And my gymnastics,' she continued. 'I play football now, Father. And my teacher says I play the violin nicely.'

'All that? My! You are doing well. Babička must be making you work very hard, practising all these things.'

'Yes, she is. Where are you, Father? When can I see you?'

'Soon, sweetheart.'

How soon?'

'Very soon. I promise.'

'You promised last time!'

'I know, but. . . .'

'I want to go to England, Father. I want to be with you again, like it used to be.'

His eyes closed with anguish. Oh, how foolish he had been! Why had he disappointed her for so long? When would it end?

Even now though, there was so little he could say, and mean. He didn't control his life. He never had done.

He swallowed hard. 'Lisa, I promise I will come for you very soon. Believe me!'

'This week?'

'Maybe next week,' he said, closing his eyes. 'I will make it happen.'

And so he would, he thought afterwards. So he bloody well would! There was nothing that mattered more to him now.

Lenka returned just after ten that night. He heard her before she reached his door, and was ready waiting for her.

She shrugged and gave him a weary smile as she entered the room. He closed the door and turned to face her.

'Anything?' he asked.

She flopped onto the bed and stretched. He waited anxiously. She was very tired. He could see that. But he needed to know.

'Lenka?'

She sighed and sat upright. 'Something is happening,' she said. 'We don't know what, but there is unusual activity. People are meeting.'

He waited.

'Your Mr Simon Mayhew flew into Prague this afternoon, unannounced.'

Harry's ears pricked up. 'Mayhew?'

'Unannounced,' she repeated for emphasis. 'He was collected and driven straight to the British Embassy, where he has remained ever since.'

'And nothing has been said?'

'Not to my minister, or to anyone in the department, no.' She shrugged and added, 'If we ask, they will say it is unofficial, a private visit. So we don't ask.'

He moved away from her and turned to the window. He opened it slightly and took a deep breath. It was very dark out there now, and bitterly cold. The weather had changed. Heavy cloud had moved in and there was the smell of snow in the air. It wasn't here yet, but it was coming; coming from the east. He had experienced it too many times before to be mistaken.

Good times, bad times, he thought wearily, the prevailing wind never let up. Never failed. Things from the east were inexorable, relentless. It had always been like that. Russia could never be discounted.

So. Mayhew was here.

'What do you make of it?' he asked, closing the window and turning back to Lenka.

She yawned. 'Not much, to be honest. But something important is going on.'

He nodded. It must be, if Mayhew had come to Prague. Mayhew was important. He didn't know what position in the intelligence world he occupied now, but whatever it was, it would be rarefied.

Mayhew had been on the rise for many years, and would have reached some significant summit by now. He had only met the guy once, many years ago, but he remembered him. He had been impressed by his cool, detached air of intelligence and general superiority. Not a man to underestimate, or alienate. They hadn't got on.

Lenka's phone vibrated softly. She pulled it out and glanced at the screen. Then she answered it, and spoke briefly. When she looked up, she was frowning.

'Trouble?'

'Not for me,' she said quickly. Then she gave him a rueful smile. 'Sorry.'

He waited.

'Two of our Russian knowns have just entered the British Embassy. Mayhew is still there.'

'Oh?'

It seemed to confirm that something big was indeed happening. If it involved Mayhew, it had to be big.

'All these things must be connected,' he suggested.

Lenka nodded. 'That's the premise we are operating on.'

'How, though? How are they connected?'

She shook her head and had nothing to add. It was a mystery.

So, he wasn't much further forward, he thought. He knew now that something important was happening, but he had no idea what. And he didn't know how, or if, it was connected to what had been happening to him.

'You were going to tell me about your daughter, I think?' Lenka said quietly.

He gave her a rueful smile. 'Was I? Was I really?'

'I think so. It's time you did, Harry.'

Still he hesitated.

'Come on,' she said. 'Let's go downstairs and see if Jan has any food he can offer us. I don't know about you, but it's a long time since I last ate.'

He glanced at his watch. Almost with surprise, he noted the time and felt hungry again himself.

'Sounds good to me,' he admitted.

Chapter Twelve

'He is here! I just know it.'

Jackson waited respectfully for the boss to explain and justify his conviction. He caught Murphy's eye and gave an almost imperceptible shake of his head to keep him quiet. The last thing he wanted was Murphy complaining about being given another runaround. They had a lot riding on this assignment: get it right and they could kiss a lot of things goodbye – including the boss.

'What? You don't agree?'

Jackson shrugged and cleared his throat. 'I have no idea,' he said, 'one way or the other.'

The look he got suggested he needed to do better than that.

'We've been chasing around Scottish islands,' he added. 'We're out of touch.'

The boss nodded, and seemed placated. 'Let me explain my thinking,' he said. 'But first, welcome back to Prague.'

'We like it here,' Murphy said, unable to stay out of it any longer.

Jackson smiled. 'What he means,' he said, 'is that we didn't like all that rain they get up there.'

'Rain? Yes, I suppose they do get rather a lot in Orkney.'

'And the rest of Scotland,' Murphy said with a shudder. 'It's as bad as Ireland. Worse, in fact.'

'Quite.'

The boss nodded and waited a moment before he began.

'Gibson will return to Prague, if he hasn't already done so, because this city is where his life has been led for many years. He is at home here, a stranger in England, and there is nowhere else he could go.'

It didn't sound much to Jackson. People running for their life didn't usually care where they went, as long as they felt safe when they got there. Their man had already been as far as Orkney, for God's sake!

'There's a million people here,' Murphy pointed out.

'And time is pressing?' the boss said. 'I know, I know. This is no time for the usual search-and-find methods. We must speed things up.'

'Maybe we should advertise for him to give himself up?' Murphy suggested, scarcely able to conceal the scorn in his voice.

Jackson winced.

The boss, surprisingly, smiled. Then he removed his glasses to polish them.

'Not a bad idea,' he said, like an old-fashioned school-master commending a favourite pupil.

He replaced his glasses and leaned forward.

'Gentlemen, we haven't time to look for Gibson. So what we need to do is bring him to us. And I know just how to do that.'

Murphy's scepticism must have been plain because the boss spoke directly to him now.

'Believe me,' he said, 'I know exactly how we can bring him in.'

Chapter Thirteen

It was late and the restaurant was quiet that evening. Jan Klaus pursed his lips in thought when Lenka spoke to him about the possibility of food. Then he disappeared into the kitchen. When he returned, a minute or two later, he brought a couple of beers and the advice that he could provide them immediately with *brambora polévka,* potato soup. Otherwise, it would take time.

'Thank you, Jan,' Lenka told him gravely. *'Polévka* will be perfect. You're an angel.'

Jan Klaus gave a little bow and Harry was astonished to see that grave face collapse into a thousand laughter lines.

'He was a friend of my father's,' Lenka said when Jan Klaus had disappeared again, 'back in the old days.'

Before 1989, he knew she meant. Before the Velvet Revolution that had ushered the Communists and Red Army out, and the year that had subsequently given Callerton the name for his new counter-espionage team.

'This restaurant,' she added, 'was one of the places where people like Vaclav Havel and my father used to meet.'

'To be dissident?'

'Exactly.' Lenka gave him a smile. 'Before the world became new again!'

He smiled himself at that.

'I've made some progress this evening,' Lenka told him. 'At least, we now know several of the people involved in the Embassy discussions.'

'So what are they talking about?'

She shrugged. 'I don't even know if anyone in my department knows that.'

'How about your minister?'

She shook her head. 'He would know only if we were able to tell him.'

'I wonder why they are meeting here?' he mused. 'Because it's neutral territory?'

'Perhaps. The Russians do all sorts of things here, as they always did. And President Klaus doesn't seem to mind too much, if at all. He is very friendly to them these days. Sometimes I think he has forgotten what it was like when they ruled our country.'

Harry nodded and chuckled. 'My impression is that he thinks he's above all that – politics. I suppose he is, constitutionally, as head of state. Coalition governments can come and go, but he sees himself as the Great Protector of the Czech Nation.'

'Something like that,' Lenka said, putting a hand to her mouth to cover a yawn. 'He's nothing like Havel, though. Maybe his ideas will work. I don't know. Tell me about your daughter, Harry.'

The change of tack caught him off guard. He sighed, but he knew he couldn't put Lenka off any longer, not if he wanted to retain her support.

'She is called Lisa.' He shrugged. 'You were right. She is 7 years old now, and looks exactly how Marika would have looked at that age.'

'So she is beautiful?'

'Of course!' He smiled. 'Despite her father, she is beautiful. If her mother could see her now, she would be very proud.'

'Marika's death was a tragedy,' Lenka said with a sigh. 'We still don't know if that car crash was a genuine accident.'

Or something else, she meant, as some still believed the road crash that had killed poor old Alexander Dubček, the country's first post-1989 president, had been. But he just nodded. By now it scarcely mattered. Nothing would bring Marika back.

'Marika wasn't the only officer we lost in those days,' Lenka added.

'Was there a pattern?'

'Not that we could see.' She shook her head and asked, 'Where does Lisa live?'

He squirmed a little over that one. They were getting close to things with the potential to hurt, things that no one at all had been told.

'I know she isn't with you,' Lenka pressed gently.

'No, she isn't.' He shook his head. 'I've told no one where she is, deliberately. I've kept her out of it.'

'I understand.'

But things had changed, apparently. Lisa's existence was known now, at least to some people.

He shrugged. 'She lives here, in Prague.'

'So that you can see her?'

'Occasionally. If it's safe.'

'And is that why you are still here?'

'A large part of it,' he admitted. 'I could probably have moved on if I had pressed for it.'

Jan Klaus arrived with their soup, some rough bread and two more glasses of beer. All talk of Lisa was suspended until he had departed.

'We believe people know she is here,' Lenka said when the conversation resumed. 'They are looking for her.'

He stared at her. 'They can't be!'

'There are indications,' she said with a shrug. 'Communications, messages, that suggest it.'

It was deeply worrying. He rubbed his face with his hands and uneasily thought it over. Could they find her? Was it possible?

'But what could anyone possibly want with her?' he asked.

Lenka shrugged. 'To put pressure on you?'

'Why?'

'Perhaps you are in somebody's way?'

He shook his head and glanced distractedly at a TV behind the bar. Manic dance scenes and unwelcome noise poured from it. He turned away and drank some beer. He was thinking furiously about what Lenka had just said.

If people were looking for Lisa, perhaps the time had come to move her. He could take her back to England with him now, which was what Lisa had long wanted. But if that was to happen, he would have to give up the idea of investigating why Unit 89 had been wiped out, never mind all thoughts of avenging Landis and the others. Well, realistically, there never had been much chance of him doing that anyway.

Lenka give a little gasp. A spoon dropped from her fingers to clatter on the floor. He glanced at her. She was staring over his shoulder.

'What is it?'

She pushed her chair back, stood up and set off across the room. He turned, stared wide-eyed at the television screen for a moment and leapt to his feet, his heart beating wildly.

Chapter Fourteen

The woman behind the bar had switched channels to catch a news bulletin. A photograph, a headshot, dominated the screen: it was of Lisa. No question about it.

Harry stumbled forward and caught the tail end of the opening commentary. A little girl was missing, believed abducted, in Prague.

The view switched to a street scene he knew only too well. He stood still, his stomach lurching, his heart pounding, and tried to concentrate on what was being said. He watched in anguish as the reporter spoke to an elderly woman, Babička. She was distraught and spoke only in monosyllables, aided by a younger woman who was described as a neighbour.

It had happened that afternoon, the younger woman said, while her friend's granddaughter was outside playing with her own daughter. Men, she said. Two men had arrived in a car and taken her.

The bulletin moved on to consider the result of an ice hockey game between Pardubice and Most. Heavy snow was forecast for much of the country. Blizzard conditions. Gas supplies from Russia. . . .

He wheeled away and sat heavily in a chair, sweating, panicking. His brain was racing out of control, doing no good at all. The nightmare he had worked for so many years to avoid had descended and paralyzed him.

'Harry? Harry, look at me!'

He felt Lenka's hands on his face. He looked up.

'Hang on, Harry!' she said softly. 'Hang on!'

His head stopped spinning. His eyes began to clear.

'I'm all right,' he said.

He wasn't, but he rallied and tried to get his brain in gear. A big question floated to the surface: how had Lenka known it was his daughter? Never mind, he thought. Leave it! Just leave it for now.

'I must speak to Babička,' he added, his voice a rasp he didn't recognize, 'and find out exactly what happened.'

'She has been living with her grandmother all this time?'

He nodded. 'It seemed the best arrangement.' He paused, took stock. 'So you were right, Lenka. About the threat. But who the hell has taken her?'

She shook her head. 'But whoever it is, we know what they want, don't we?'

He didn't bother replying. The kidnappers wanted him. It was obvious. He was the last piece in the jigsaw, last man standing.

Back in his room, he stared out of the window while Lenka worked her phone. She was trying to find out more, but he didn't bother listening. She would tell him anything she learned. His mind, surprisingly, was focused and cool now. He had got over the shock, the dreadful, gut-gripping fear that had come with seeing Lisa's photograph on the television screen. He knew now what he had to do.

First, he had to speak to Babička. He had to hear directly from her what had happened. Then. . . . Then he would have to trade – himself for Lisa.

Lenka finished her phone calls.

'Anything?' he asked, looking round.

She shook her head. 'Not yet.' She scrutinized him. 'How are you, Harry?'

'I'm OK. I've just been working out what to do. First, I need to talk to Babička.'

'Yes?' Lenka looked dubious. 'Perhaps it would be better if I spoke to her? They may be waiting for you to turn up.'

'She wouldn't speak to you, Lenka. She doesn't know you. It has to be me.'

'Then we should go together,' she insisted.

'Is that wise – for you?'

She shrugged. 'Is any of what we do completely wise?'

'Probably not, no.' He hesitated and then added, 'I'll phone her first.'

'And is that wise?'

Of course it wasn't! He shook his head, irritated with himself.

'What's wrong with me? I'm not thinking straight.'

'You have had a terrible shock, Harry. That's all. There is nothing wrong with you. But two heads are better than one in a situation like this.'

He glanced at his watch. Gone eleven. Late for Babička, but she wouldn't be sleeping tonight, any more than he would be himself.

'Let's go,' he said.

Babička lived in Holešovice, once a separate town, way out in the north-eastern part of Prague. They drove there in Lenka's little Skoda, travelling fast. They crossed the Vltava via Čechův Most, one of the big bridges, and sped along the northern bank of the river, leaving the bright lights of the central area behind. The roads were quiet. As midnight approached, the city was drifting off to sleep.

The old house where Babička had lived all her married life was a detached, two-storey building that had long been divided into two apartments, one up, one down. It was shabby, run-down even, but spacious and still pleasant. Better to live there than in a modern tower block, he had always thought. The surrounding garden, with its mature shrubs and trees, added to the house's character. Lisa had been fortunate to live in such a place, as had her mother been before her.

Lenka stopped at the end of the road, near the exhibition ground containing the Bruselsky Pavilion, which he knew had something to do with the 1958 Brussels World Fair. They considered how best to approach the house. It was possible, likely even, that it was being watched by somebody.

'Perhaps you could get in at the back, through the garden?' Lenka suggested.

He shook his head. 'Not in the dark. It's jungle down there. Fifty years' worth.'

'But if you approach the house directly, from the front, you might just as well give yourself up.'

He grimaced, knowing she was right. 'You're going to have to go instead, Lenka.'

'Yes, but how do we persuade her to trust me?'

'Just tell her Mr Harry needs to speak to her. That's what she usually calls me. Say he doesn't trust the phone, and is waiting in the exhibition ground. And tell her Marika was your friend. Keep it simple,' he added. 'We don't want to risk confusing her.'

'Where exactly shall we meet in the exhibition ground? It is a big place.'

'Don't worry about that. Just get there. I'll come to you.'

He left the car and slipped into the shadow cast by a high hedge. He waited until Lenka drove away. Then he turned and walked back to the exhibition ground.

The place was empty, deserted. Not entirely dark, but lit only by occasional and feeble street lamps. He walked across the vast parking area near the entrance, empty acres of tarmac stretching away before him. In the near distance, there were buildings that could have been part of a funfair, and beyond them he could see the outline of the main conference hall against the night sky. All was in darkness now.

The night was bitterly cold. He shivered, pulled up the hood of his jacket and headed for the shadowy buildings around the edge of the parking area. He slipped, recovered his balance; realized a veneer of ice had formed on the wet surface of the tarmac.

Looking for shelter, he moved into the doorway of a lapidarium, a museum for stones and gems, and stood there to wait. They wouldn't be long. Either Babička would come instantly, or not at all. If she was there, he didn't think she would take much persuading.

A breeze stirred, catching something loose at the corner of the building, making it rattle. Guttering, perhaps. A few bits of white fluff floated into the doorway. Then more came. He glanced up and saw the stars disappearing. It looked as if the forecast was right, and the warnings justified. The snow was arriving a little early this year. He shivered again and wriggled his shoulders. It was cold. He was cold.

Ten minutes later, a car turned into the entrance. He tensed. It could be Lenka's Skoda, but he needed to be sure. The headlights swept across the empty tarmac, reflecting off patches of ice and gleaming pools of winter rain. The car crept slowly into the centre of the open space, circled, and drew to a halt outside a kiosk that was shuttered up for the winter. *Zmrzlina* ice-cream: a giant white cone, with red and yellow swirls spiralling down it. And snowflakes, drifting down more heavily now, just before Lenka cut the lights.

He waited a little longer. But no other vehicle came through the entrance. It looked as if they had not been followed. Either the watchers had been taken by surprise, or they were just short-handed, and had no one available to follow when Babička left the house unexpectedly at such a late hour.

He strode quickly across to the car, ducking his head against a sudden flurry of snowflakes. Lenka spotted him coming and opened her door to climb out.

'All right?' he asked.

'I think so. She was still up. A bit traumatized, I think. I'll let you speak to her. Snow?' she added, looking round and giving a little shiver. 'Already?'

'What a country!' he said.

He got into the car and closed the door, leaving Lenka outside to keep watch.

'Babi!' he said gently. 'How are you?'

She turned to him and he wrapped her in his arms. She gave a little sob and said, 'Oh, Mr Harry! I am so sorry.'

'Ssh! It wasn't your fault, Babi. I shouldn't have left her with you so long.'

She sniffled and tried to compose herself. 'Everything was fine. Life was normal. Then – poof!'

He waited for her to calm down. Then he released her and gently took hold of her hand.

'Tell me,' he said gently. 'Just tell me what happened.'

'First, I have something for you. They left an envelope with my neighbour's little girl.'

He took the envelope from her and tore it open. In the faint glow from the instrument panel, he read the typed message on the small sheet of paper. It was brief and to the point:

Four o'clock tomorrow afternoon. The girl will be at the entrance to St Peter and St Paul in Všehrad.

All was indisputably clear. There was no room at all for uncertainty. It really was him they wanted.

'Go on,' he said, turning back to Babička. 'Exactly what happened?'

There wasn't much to tell. Lisa had been playing outside on the street with her friend from a nearby house. The girls played together most days. This time they had been using their scooters. It was a safe street, normally. Not much traffic to speak of. Only residents' cars. So Babi had never had qualms about Lisa playing there.

'She is a growing child,' she explained. 'She cannot be kept indoors or in the garden all the time.'

'No, of course not. You have looked after her very well.'

Babi sighed. 'She was so happy, Mr Harry, knowing you were near, and that she would see you soon.'

He nodded. 'What happened?' he pressed again.

'I did not see it myself. Terezka, my neighbour's daughter, said a big black car arrived, and stopped. Two men got out. They picked Lisa up and put her in the car. Then they gave the other girl the envelope. That is all.'

Babi sniffled. He squeezed her hand gently. He didn't blame her; she had performed wonders, looking after Lisa alone these past several years. It hadn't been easy for her, not least because she was no longer a well woman. Time had caught up with her.

'We'll get her back,' he said. 'Don't worry, Babi.'

She looked round at him, her face tear-streaked in the reflected light. 'You think so?'

He nodded. 'Don't worry,' he repeated. 'I know who has her, and I know what they want. I'll get her back.'

He was sure of that, at least. He had no idea how he would do it, but he was certain that he would. Any other outcome was unthinkable while he still had breath in his body.

Chapter Fifteen

It was too cold to sit in the car and do nothing but wait. So every once in a while, Murphy turned on the engine, and the heater. The trouble with that, apart from the noise, was that the warm air fogged up all the windows. But the alternative was to die of hypothermia.

Jackson blew into his cupped hands and said, 'Switch it on again.'

Murphy turned the key. Engine and heater came back to life.

'Do you think he'll come tonight?' Murphy asked.

'He'll come.' Jackson nodded emphatically and added, 'I agree with the boss. He'll want to know what happened.'

When Murphy didn't respond, Jackson said, 'What do you think?'

'I think it's fucking cold!'

Jackson chuckled. 'Orkney was too rainy, and now it's too cold!'

'Why don't they run to Mexico any more?' Murphy said plaintively. 'That was a good place to go.'

'Yeah. It was a pity we found him as fast as we did, that guy. I wouldn't have minded if it had taken another month. Mexico, eh? Good country.'

'Maybe we should go there? You know – afterwards, when we get the money?'

Jackson frowned and pretended to give it a little thought. 'I don't think so,' he said reluctantly. 'The place is a war zone these days, what with the drug gangs and the government attacking each other. Switch the wipers on a minute, can you?' he added.

'See something?'

Jackson peered through the windscreen as the wipers started working. After a few moments, he shook his head and settled back in his seat. 'I don't think so,' he said. 'But it's started to snow.'

'What we needed,' Murphy said.

Jackson wasn't sure what he'd seen, the windscreen was so fogged up. Had it been movement?

'Tell you what,' he said to Murphy. 'Why don't you wait outside? You'll have a better view.'

'And you wait here, in the warm and the dry?'

'That's it.'

'I don't think so, thanks. I've got a better idea. Why don't we call it a night, and clear off?'

'Soon,' Jackson said. 'Just give it a bit longer.'

The snow became heavier. Murphy wondered if anyone else in Prague was as stupid as them. There were times when all the money in the world didn't seem worth it.

'Damn!' Jackson said, leaning forward. 'How did she get out?'

Murphy peered hard through the windscreen and saw what Jackson meant. An old woman was closing her gate and turning to walk up the garden path. There was no doubt who it was.

'There must be another way in and out,' Jackson said,

tapping the dashboard with his fingers. 'Gibson could have been and gone while we've been sitting here.'

'It's hard to see any damn thing in this weather,' Murphy said, already planning what they could say to the boss. 'But we'll get him tomorrow, if not tonight.'

Jackson nodded. 'Let's go. I've had enough of this.'

Chapter Sixteen

'Tomorrow,' he said, clutching the grab handle. 'They want to meet in Vyšehrad.'

Lenka nodded and then swore as the car slid sideways and turned round to face backwards.

'This snow!' she exclaimed.

'You're driving,' he said with a grin.

The conditions were bad, and rapidly getting worse. The radio was warning continually now of blizzard conditions sweeping the country. The forecasters had been right, he thought, even if it was a bit early in the winter for weather like this.

'We should have listened to the forecast,' Lenka said.

He shrugged. It wouldn't have made any difference. They would still have come. He would, at least, and he couldn't imagine that Lenka would have let him come alone.

'You watched Babička go inside the house?' he asked.

'Of course. Men were watching from a parked car, but we managed to get past them both times.'

He hoped Babi would be all right in what remained of the night. She ought to be. All she had to do now was wait – and worry.

'What time tomorrow?' Lenka asked.

'Four in the afternoon.'

'Not the morning? That's strange.'

He had wondered about that himself. What it seemed to mean was that they wanted to minimize the risk of the meeting being observed. At that time of day, going dark, and in that particular place, it was unlikely there would be onlookers. Especially now the weather had turned. It didn't augur well for his own survival prospects, but that couldn't be helped. He had no choice. He had to go. They would know that.

'They'. Whoever 'they' were, he thought bitterly.

He assumed it was the same people – his people – who had been hunting him all along, ever since the attack on Unit 89. Jackson and Murphy, and whoever was pulling their strings. He couldn't imagine who that might be.

'Perhaps we should stay somewhere closer to the venue?' Lenka suggested, peering hard through the windscreen. 'Movement will be difficult tomorrow, if this keeps up.'

He was glad of the observation. Thinking about who was hunting him – and who now held Lisa – was too difficult, and too painful.

'You're right,' he said.

It would be utter chaos tomorrow as people struggled to get to and from work, and as the authorities were stretched to cope with mountains of snow, blocked roads, abandoned vehicles, and trams and buses going nowhere fast. Not to mention people stranded in nowhere land.

'There's a hotel nearby,' he said. 'The Barbican?'

'I know it.'

'Let's make for that.'

They travelled on, their speed dropping drastically as the snow built up on roads that wouldn't be ploughed for hours.

They could hear the wind roaring above the screaming of the Skoda's engine. It was more like being out on the Russian steppes than near the centre of a sophisticated European city.

'We're not dressed for this weather,' Lenka remarked, as if the fact had only just occurred to her.

'We'll manage.'

Somehow they would, he thought. He would have to do some sort of recce anyway, whatever the inadequacy of their clothing. There was no way he was going to turn up for the meeting tomorrow without doing that. He wondered what the abductors' plan would be for the meeting, but he soon gave that up. Speculation was pointless until he had done a recce.

They travelled on for a while without speaking. The weather worsened. Lenka concentrated hard on her driving, pressing the car on through the deepening snow, unable to see far in front even with the wipers going full speed. He avoided distracting her with idle conversation.

The snow was piling up on the road, and there was a constant roaring noise as the bottom of the car ploughed through it. He began to wonder how much further they would get before the car stopped, finally stuck, and they had to start walking.

They crossed the Vltava by the Čechův Bridge again and turned to run along the embankment. The snow was not so deep here, the road sheltered by the massive buildings fronting the river.

'Whoops!' Lenka cried as the car turned sideways again and slid across the road. 'Sorry about that.'

'We're nearly there,' he said to encourage her. 'Keep it going a little bit further.'

They managed another couple of blocks. Then they hit

deep snow in a wide-open intersection and the car dug into it and stopped. The engine died. Lenka tried to restart it, but without success. He guessed too much snow had built up inside the engine compartment. Nothing in there would turn now, and no spark ignite.

'That's it,' she said, turning to him with a shrug. 'We're walking from now on.'

He looked around. He couldn't see out of the rear window for packed snow. The side windows were fogged up. All he could see through the windscreen was driving snow, illuminated by the background glow from neon street lamps. The only sound was the shrieking of the wind as it drove yet more snow hard against this puny obstacle in its way.

'Right,' he said, not looking forward to what had to come next. 'Let's get on with it.'

He opened his door and was immediately hit in the face by a blast of snow. He stumbled out and doubled over for a moment to catch his breath. When he straightened up, he saw that Lenka had got out on the other side and was foraging on the back seat. He joined her in salvaging a few things that might prove useful.

Then they began walking, trudging, head down, through snow that was now up over their knees. Progress was slow and hard work, made more difficult by the relentless wind screaming in their faces and hammering them with snow.

'About a kilometre!' he shouted to encourage Lenka.

She seemed to nod but didn't turn to look at him, still less to answer him. Ten minutes, he thought. If they survived that long!

The temperature, given the wind chill factor, was probably off any scale he had ever encountered. He held an arm across his face to lessen the impact of the driving snow and battled on, sometimes catching hold of Lenka and pulling her along when she faltered.

They reached the Barbican at last; there were lights inside. Not many, but some. The big front door wouldn't open, though, and no one came when he rang the bell. He kept his finger on the button for a couple of minutes, but nothing happened. He grew frantic, closing his eyes against the searing cold.

'It's no good!' Lenka shouted in his ear. 'Harry, we must go!'

'Go? Go where, for God's sake!'

Frostbite was a real danger. His face felt cracked. His ears and fingers were numb.

'Harry!' She pulled at his arm.

'We'll have to break in,' he shouted.

'No! We can't. We must go somewhere else. Come!'

He took his finger off the button and reluctantly turned around. Lenka was already moving away. Even more reluctantly, he followed her.

They ploughed across what once must have been a wide road, but was now a wasteland. They made their way up a narrow lane, heading into the bitterly icy wind and the driving snow, going he had no idea where. He just followed Lenka, who was forging on, head down. He hoped to God she knew what she was doing – and where she was going.

They came to a rock wall at the end of the lane. He stared at it despairingly. They were out of the wind here, but they needed more than that small comfort.

Lenka foraged with a bare hand in a recess in the wall for a few moments. Then she moved sideways and worked at something else. When she took hold with both hands and began to pull, he joined her. It was, he realized with growing interest, some kind of door. Once started, it moved fairly easily, opening to expose a dark interior.

Lenka stepped inside and a moment later, a low-intensity light came on. She had found a switch. Now she pulled him in after her. He turned to help her close the door, which was heavy and appeared to be made of thick steel plate. It shut with a loud clunk. The noise of the blizzard ceased instantly.

Harry stood still for a moment, catching his breath. Then he straightened up.

'Is this place what I assume it is?' he asked, wiping away snow-melt from his face.

'Probably.'

Lenka turned to a panel on the wall and began pressing switches. A generator started up. More lights came on. He could see then that they were in a long passage, with doors on both sides at regular intervals.

'A nuclear shelter?' he said wonderingly.

'Yes. One my department keeps for its own use.'

He shook his head, gazing around and marvelling at the scale of the work that had been accomplished here. But he knew the facility wasn't exceptional. Such places were all over Prague, or had been during the Cold War years, enough to provide shelter in an emergency for hundreds of thousands of people. Not the entire population of the city, perhaps, but a very large part of it.

'That's better!' Lenka turned and gave him a crooked smile. 'Not five-star, exactly, but. . . .'

'But out of the wind and the snow. That's more than enough.'

She grinned. 'Come on. Let's get sorted out.'

She led the way into one of the rooms off the main

corridor. The accommodation was pretty basic, but just what refugees like them needed. Bare concrete floors perhaps, but bunk beds and stacks of quilts and blankets. Shelves holding canned food and containers of water. Waste receptacles and cooking stoves, and a couple of portaloos.

Everything they needed, he thought, looking round with amazement. It was wonderful. Perfect.

'It even feels warm,' he said, surprised. 'Or is it just me? I would have expected a place like this to be cold and damp.'

'No. It is dry here. And caves have a constant temperature that in winter is higher than the temperature outdoors. Also, these shelters have pressure control systems to keep out poison gas and fumes. Normally they're switched off, but we keep this one going. Don't ask me why!'

He smiled. 'I wouldn't dream of it. I'm just so pleased you knew this place existed.'

'Oh, we all know that – where to go in an emergency.'

He opened his coat and began to peel it off. 'I'm warming up already.'

'My feet aren't,' Lenka complained. 'Nor my hands.'

'Let me see.'

She held out her hands. He studied them and gently pressed them to stir the blood circulation.

'They're just cold,' he said. 'It's not frostbite. What about your feet?'

'Just cold, too,' she said dismissively. 'We weren't out long enough to have serious problems. Now, are you hungry?'

He shook his head. 'Something to drink, though? Water, perhaps.'

'Hot coffee?'

'Now you're talking!'

Lenka began fiddling with a small camping stove. He sat

on a bottom bunk bed and took off his shoes. His feet were wet and cold. He dried them with a towel and massaged them. Then he stuffed his shoes with paper he found amongst the kitchen supplies.

'We should do the same with yours,' he advised when Lenka looked to see what he was doing. 'They'll dry faster.'

Lenka chuckled. 'My shoes need radiators in them!'

But she slipped her shoes off and handed them over. He dealt with them, then he took the steaming mug of coffee she handed him, and made way for her to join him on the bunk bed.

'What are you thinking now?' she asked after a moment.

'About tomorrow.' He sipped the coffee. 'I'm wondering how it will go. There are no handover arrangements specified in the letter. Just the instruction to meet outside the church.'

'What does that tell you?'

'It's not good.' He grimaced. 'Either they are total amateurs or else a handover isn't really intended.'

'They will try to kill you,' Lenka said bleakly, 'like the others.'

He nodded. He was under no illusions. 'Lisa, too, probably.'

Lenka said nothing to that. There was nothing easy that could be said.

He glanced at his watch. 2.30 now. Plenty of time to look for a solution. Time to get some sleep, even.

'It's no good asking for support,' Lenka said thoughtfully. 'If they see you are not alone, or if they suspect a trap, they will not appear. It must be us alone, I think. Just you and I.'

He nodded. She was right.

'They can drive in, can't they?' he asked.

'Yes. From near the metro station. Through the big

archway, the main entrance.'

On top of the hill, he thought, on top of the hill they were at the bottom of right now. That's where the church was. And the medieval battlements.

He knew that Vyšehrad was, or had been in earlier times, a fortified hill, as well as a sacred site. It had been occupied for a thousand years or more, and sometimes preferred by the kings of Bohemia to Hradčany and the more modern castle complex that had become the centre of government. Folklore even had it that Vyšehrad was the original Slav settlement in these lands.

Generations of fortifications had been built, destroyed, and rebuilt over the centuries. The massive walls now dated mostly from the sixteenth and seventeenth centuries, and the Baroque era, as did the church and the cemetery on top of the hill. So too, did the labyrinth of tunnels that had once serviced the great guns and allowed defenders to move about more easily and safely.

'Is this part of the ancient tunnel system?' he asked, glancing up at the vaulted ceiling.

Lenka shrugged. 'Who knows?' she said. 'Who can tell?'

'Does it connect with other tunnels?'

'Not that I know of. But I don't think so. This shelter is supposed to be sealed and self-contained.'

He nodded. That sounded about right. A self-contained complex in the heart of an ancient fortified hill. They should be safe enough here for the night.

'I'm going to have to turn up for the meeting tomorrow,' he said slowly, thinking it through. 'Otherwise they won't bring Lisa.'

'They may not bring her anyway, Harry.'

He knew that. But he had no alternative. None at all. He

didn't even know who the 'they' were who were holding his daughter. Everything remained guesswork.

Chapter Seventeen

The blizzard passed on overnight, although they didn't know that until they opened the shelter door the next morning and found the sun shining out of a vivid blue sky. It was very cold still, but the snow had stopped. Ploughs were busy on the street below and traffic was beginning to move again.

'I'd better see if I can rescue my car,' Lenka said.

Harry nodded. 'I want to recce the hill. Let's meet back at the Barbican at twelve.'

Vyšehrad was a big hill covering a wide area, but there was only one way into it by road. He made his way up the wooded hillside to that entrance, a big, arched, stone gateway through the historic wall. He walked through the archway and on past several rather grand ancient buildings. One was in use as some sort of school for handicapped youngsters.

He kept going, past the historic cemetery where so many famous Czech artists and writers were buried, and on to the wide-open space around the church of St Peter and St Paul. A well-tended lawn in summer, now it was an arctic scene deep in snow.

He spent a few minutes trudging with difficulty round the ramparts on the perimeter of the hill top, a stone walkway that gave spectacular views over the Vltava and much of the city.

Frequently, he glanced back at the entrance to the church, where he was supposed to meet Lisa's abductors. If he stood there waiting, no one would be able to approach him unseen. On the other hand, a very ordinary sort of shot would be able to pick him off from any number of vantage points around the walls. It wouldn't take a sniper to do it.

He grimaced and looked around. The chances were, there would be no witnesses either. There wouldn't be many visitors up here on a day like this, especially in the fading light of late afternoon, with quite possibly more snow on the way and the temperature way below freezing. He would be as exposed, and as safe, as a target in a shooting gallery.

A glance up at the lowering sky strengthened his expectation of more snow soon. Whether or not it would be a return of blizzard conditions, clouds were moving in already. He shivered. New snow didn't feel far away at all.

He studied the open area in front of the church for a few more minutes, seeing nothing to change his mind or to reduce his forebodings. They – whoever 'they' were – were unlikely to be interested in any sort of exchange. Not really. They simply wanted him dead. Lisa would be collateral damage, a bait that had drawn him into the open when they couldn't catch him by other means. Leaving her alive afterwards would be seen as a pointless risk.

There wasn't much more he could do here, either now or in – he glanced at his watch – six hours' time. He turned to retrace his footsteps, back to the main entrance to Vyšehrad.

One good thing he had discovered was that there was no reason for the meeting not to go ahead as scheduled. The road up the hill to the entrance was negotiable, despite the snow. Already, a delivery van had made it to the school for handicapped children. It stood there now, steaming in the ferocious cold.

He made his way down the hill and met Lenka at the hotel. She had managed to rescue her car without too much difficulty. There had even been time for her to buy them both some winter boots and woolly socks. In the hotel coffee lounge, with no one near, Harry surreptitiously changed his footwear.

'Perfect!' he announced with a grateful smile. 'Another couple of days and my feet might be warm and dry again.'

'You English!' Lenka said scornfully. 'You have no idea how to survive a Czech winter.'

'What do you mean! I just wasn't ready for it. It's scarcely even November.'

Lenka was unimpressed. 'In this country,' she said solemnly, 'one must be prepared – for anything.'

He grinned and sipped his coffee.

'You haven't changed much,' he said. 'You always were a good teacher. Especially in the early days, when I knew nothing about this country.'

She smiled. 'It was fun, wasn't it? Those days after the Velvet Revolution, when your people came to help us, and we helped you. They were so . . . so exciting! There's no other word for it. The Red Army and the Communists gone, we had our country back.'

He nodded and smiled back at her. Yes, indeed, he reflected. Fun and exciting. Even more so as he got to know Lenka's colleague, Marika.

'Great days,' he said with a nostalgic sigh. 'Great times.'

For a few quiet moments, just a few, it was good to remember them.

*

They stayed in the hotel to eat a quick lunch and make their plans for the afternoon. Lenka listened carefully to what he had in mind and made one or two suggestions herself. Then she departed to collect a couple of essential items, leaving him to get through the next couple of hours as best he could.

He ordered another coffee and turned to the newspapers in the hotel lounge. Whatever their nationality and language, they all led on gas supply problems. The arctic weather that had been forecast to reach across Europe, and that had now arrived in Prague, had made the story inevitable. People everywhere were struggling to stay warm and to keep things moving.

Russian gas was having trouble getting through again, he read, one reason being the recurrence of the argument between Russia and Ukraine over transit prices. Ukraine was declining to pay the world price for Russian gas. So Russia was warning once again that gas supplies to Ukraine would be cut, and Ukraine was responding that it would take the gas it needed from the pipeline traversing its territory. It was not a new story. Not a new situation either. Until other conduits for Russian gas exports were open, it was a story that would not go away.

He shook his head wearily. The last time this problem had erupted, people had died in Romania, Slovakia and elsewhere. It was no fun being downline from a main source of energy when cold weather was coming and the big boys who controlled the supply were arguing with each other.

He put aside the Czech news-sheets and turned to a couple of the English-language American papers. He skimmed through the leaders without much interest. Then he spotted a story on the inside of the *Christian Science Monitor* that made him sit up straight. He read it through quickly, and paused for thought. Then he went back and read it again, more carefully this time, all the while making links and connections.

The country at the tail end of the pipeline from Russia was, of course, the UK. The European country with the smallest storage facilities for gas was also the UK. The country with the smallest reserves. . . .

The UK had five-days' supply of gas in store. The coldest weather for a long time was forecast. Conclusion: the UK was very vulnerable. In fact, it was teetering on the edge of disaster. There was a very real danger that the lights would go out soon in hospitals as well as homes, in factories as well as the City of London.

He laid the paper aside and wondered if this was the answer he had been seeking. Was this what the UK wanted very badly from Russia: an assured gas supply?

Was this what the intense discussions in Prague, involving even the Secret Service, were about right now? Was it possible that this was the explanation at last of why Unit 89 had been wiped off the board? The quid pro quo?

You want more gas? Well, we can certainly give you that. But first, you must eliminate your Russian counter-espionage team in Central Europe. OK?

He could imagine the answer wouldn't have been very long in coming, and that it would have been reluctant acquiescence. Too much was at stake for it to have been otherwise. It wouldn't be the only concession, of course; the unit wasn't that important. But it could be part of a package the Russians were demanding in return for boosting their gas exports to the UK.

The more he thought about it, the more he believed this

might well be the key he had been seeking to recent events. Cally had even tried to flag it up for him by circling the headline in his paper about Siberian gas. Unit 89? What were half a dozen lives when weighed against the numbers that would die, and the chaos that would follow, if the UK's energy supply system was found wanting in the teeth of a blizzard?

It all made sense, and it was almost a relief to have stumbled upon the probable explanation for the terrible things that had been happening.

Lenka returned mid-afternoon. They left together then, to drive up the hill to the meeting venue. They parked the car just outside the main entrance to Vyšehrad and made their way on foot through the archway.

'What do you think?' Harry asked after a quick survey of the area immediately beyond the entrance.

Lenka looked round and shrugged. 'We will see.'

'Happy to take part?'

'Of course.' She gave him a stern look. 'You didn't think any differently, did you?'

He shook his head and gave her a hug.

The plan was simple, the preparations needed few. From his position, he could scarcely detect the stinger beneath its dusting of snow. He was sure no driver of an oncoming vehicle would see anything there at all.

Lenka had positioned her car near the entrance to the archway, and was prepared to simulate a stalled vehicle. Any approaching vehicle would have to wait for her to manoeuvre her car out of the way, and that would give him time to remove the stinger if the vehicle was not the one they were anticipating. At this time of day, in these conditions, he didn't really expect that to be necessary.

So he would confront them here, before they had even got into the Vyšehrad citadel. It was a better option than the one he had been given.

It was an anxious wait. He tried not to think about Lisa. This was all about her but he couldn't afford to dwell on thoughts of her. He wanted no distractions, nothing to mar his judgement and cloud his perceptions. He needed to be cool and able to act decisively when the time came; survival for them both was at stake.

Twenty minutes later, he heard Lenka working the starter motor hard. It meant they were here. She would have beeped the horn if it hadn't been them.

The Skoda's engine fired and caught eventually. It revved hard as she clumsily manoeuvred the car out of the way.

Any second now! He pulled the Glock pistol clear of his jacket, glanced at it and braced himself.

A big black car eased through the archway. The Jaguar again. So it was them. There was scarcely time to register the fact before the front tyres hit the stinger and popped. The front end of the car slumped onto the snow.

He stared hard at the car. Darkened windows. He couldn't see through them. Was she in there?

Both front doors opened: Jackson and Murphy again. They appeared, one on each side of the car, guns in hand, looking around, on full alert. Jackson stepped to the front of the car, saw what the problem was, and wheeled around with a warning shout to Murphy.

Harry stayed where he was, behind a stone pillar. As yet, they didn't know where the attack was coming from, or if indeed one was coming at all – and he didn't know if they had brought Lisa. He grimaced. He hadn't anticipated this situation.

Jackson started to move in his direction.

'Stop right there, Jackson! No further forward. You too, Murphy!'

'Gibson!' Jackson said, not fazed at all.

'Have you got the girl?'

'What girl's that?'

He could see them both. Murphy was edging sideways round the back of the Jaguar, while Jackson did the talking. He needed to stop Murphy moving.

'Murphy!'

Jackson edged forward another step. Harry fired, and missed. Jackson returned fire and dived back behind the car.

A bullet whined off the pillar. Murphy's contribution.

Then Lenka opened up from somewhere in the archway, forcing both men to scramble for shelter at the front of the car.

Harry grimaced and spat into the snow. Stalemate. And he still didn't know if they had brought Lisa.

He heard a vehicle approaching at speed, powering up the hill, sirens blaring and flashing lights brightening the evening sky. The archway was suddenly full of noise and light. A police car edged into view: city police. Initially on a routine visit, he guessed, but then responding to the sound of gunshots as dusk fell across the city.

Two uniformed men got out of the car, weapons in hand. A radio crackled. Orders were shouted by megaphone as the cops moved alongside the Jaguar. Risky for them, but the shooting had stopped. Too late for Jackson and Murphy to press on. They would have to resort to being outraged diplomats.

There were other figures moving about in the background now, attracted by the commotion. Vyšehrad was apparently not as deserted as it had seemed. A group of figures stumbled down the road from the school, one of them using crutches. A woman, somewhere, began screaming.

Harry moved out from behind the pillar, preparing to explain himself. Then a rear door of the Jaguar opened and a small form emerged, straightened and ran towards him.

'*Tati!* Daddy!'

His heart skipped. She was here! He gasped and dashed forward. He met her halfway, scooped her up in his arms and ran through the archway.

Lenka called to him, and led off down a narrow path deep in snow. He ran after her, Lisa secure in his arms.

Chapter Eighteen

The snow was deep on the hillside, in places waist-deep. They ploughed through it at breakneck pace, Lenka leading the way. Lisa clung to Harry like a marsupial pup, eyes tight shut and gripping hard.

He glanced over his shoulder a couple of times. There was no pursuit – yet!

Keep going, keep going!

On a particularly steep section, he slipped, crashed onto his back and slid out of control until he thudded into a tree. Lisa yelped with fright. He held tight on to her.

Lenka yelled a query. He had no breath left. He just waved her on and struggled back to his feet.

He guessed she was leading them back to the shelter. It was close and it had everything they needed; most of all, it offered security, if only they could reach it.

Lower down the hillside, it was night now, and would have been quite dark but for the light from street lamps reflecting from the snow. Their pace slowed, but they kept going. There was no halt until they reached the entrance to the shelter.

Lenka stopped, glanced around and then opened the door. As he stumbled inside, he saw her going backwards, sweeping away their tell-tale footprints from the snow. He let her do it. His arms were killing him. But when Lisa opened her eyes and looked at him, he could have carried her back up the hill and down again once more.

It was wonderfully warm in the shelter, even more so in the room they had used previously. He hadn't realized until then how cold he had got up on the hill. It had been a long wait, up there in the snow.

He stooped to set Lisa down on a bunk bed, but she wouldn't let go. Gently, he teased her fingers loose, soothing her with kisses and gentle words.

'How is she?' Lenka asked anxiously as she entered the room.

He wasn't sure. He straightened up, his eyes never leaving Lisa's. She stared at him without expression for a few more moments. Then her eyes came to life and she began to smile. He smiled back, relieved, almost overwhelmed.

'I was going to say traumatized,' he said softly over his shoulder to Lenka, 'but that's wrong. She's fine, I think.'

He stooped to kiss the little girl again. Lisa laced her arms around his neck, ignoring his protests. 'I knew you would come for me,' she said happily, shyly. 'I just knew!'

'Of course you did. Of course I would. How are you, sweetheart?'

'Hot,' she said, starting to unfasten her coat. 'Now I am.'

He smiled and turned back to Lenka. 'Thank you,' he said, hugging her, too. 'You were wonderful.'

'We were lucky,' she said simply.

And he knew that to be true. The plan, such as it was, would have stalled in its tracks if the police officers had not appeared when they did, and even earlier if Lenka hadn't taken it upon herself to open fire on Murphy.

He shook his head at the memory of the crazy scene up

there.

'I couldn't believe it when the police arrived. How lucky was that? I'd thought the place was deserted.'

'It would have been if I hadn't called them.'

He stared at her.

'I guessed we might need backup. Those were not ordinary police officers, Harry. They were some of my colleagues, and eager to take part. We're all tired of foreigners creating havoc on our sovereign territory.'

He shook his head with astonishment.

'Thank you again – even more!'

'Now, young lady,' Lenka said, brushing past him. 'What would you like? Something to eat and drink?'

Lisa smiled uncertainly. Then she frowned and looked round with wide-open eyes, as if seeing the place for the first time.

'Where are we?' she asked dubiously.

'A safe place,' Lenka assured her. 'We are inside a mountain. No one can reach us here.'

The eyes opened even wider. 'Inside a mountain? Wow!'

'It is a very secret place. You must not tell anyone about it.'

Lisa shook her head with a silent promise. 'Do they have hot chocolate here?' she asked.

'Possibly. Would you like some?'

Lisa nodded.

'I'll see what I can do.'

Lenka turned away. She poured water from a plastic bottle into a kettle and put the kettle on a camping stove to heat. Then she began to search the shelves for hot chocolate powder.

'Coffee, Harry?'

He nodded appreciatively and sat down, holding Lisa close. Just then, he really wasn't capable of much more, and he didn't want to do anything else anyway.

Lisa seemed unharmed. That was something to be grateful for. A lot, actually. Perhaps she would carry unfortunate memories in her head for a while, but otherwise she seemed fine. To Jackson and Murphy, she would have been of little consequence. They had not hurt her deliberately but they would have snuffed her out, as well as him, without concern when the time came. That thought made the present moment seem even more precious.

Lisa took the mug of hot chocolate and sipped cautiously until she had established that it was to her liking. Lenka gave Harry a complicit smile. He winked. All was well in their cave. As Lenka had said, they had been lucky. It made a welcome change.

Only their watches gave any indication of the passage of time, but pass it did. A couple of hours later, Lenka looked outside and returned to say that the wind had got up and it was snowing heavily again. There was no need for her to add that it would be best to remain where they were for the night.

Lisa was excited, understandably so, but eventually she grew tired and struggled to keep her eyes open. They put her to bed in a sleeping bag on the bottom bunk, where they were sitting. As long as she could see and feel her father's presence, she seemed content. She soon fell asleep, and even began to snore.

Lenka chuckled. 'Just listen to her!'

Harry smiled back. 'A regular little old lady, isn't she?'

'You're lucky to have her, Harry. I'm so glad we were able to rescue her.'

'It was a worrying situation,' he admitted.

'If you had gone to the meeting as they wanted, we

wouldn't be sitting here now.'

There was no need to say anything in response. The reality was inescapable.

He nodded agreement. 'By the way, I think I know what those discussions at the embassy are about. And it might explain why the decision was taken to eliminate Unit 89.'

'Go on,' she said, curious.

He told her. He told her about the looming gas crisis, particularly in Britain.

'It's enough, isn't it?' she said wearily. 'It would be just like the Russians to seize the opportunity to press their advantage. I wonder what else they have demanded.'

He shook his head. 'Probably a long list of things. They could demand almost anything right now. The potential consequences of the country not having enough power don't bear thinking about.

'What are half a dozen lives, already sworn to defend Queen and country,' he added bitterly, 'compared with that catastrophe in waiting?'

Lenka nodded. 'I used to think,' she said wearily, 'that lives lived in the shadows, like ours, were worthwhile.'

'And now?'

'Now I no longer know. We don't seem to achieve much.'

That about summed it up for him, too. Especially in recent years. What good had Unit 89 done? What did it matter that there were Russian spies in central Europe? And what difference would it make now that Unit 89 was no longer there to watch them?

'Well, I've made up my mind,' he said. 'I'm out of it now. I can't stop them coming after me, but I'm going to make damned sure they don't find me – us, I mean,' he added, nodding towards Lisa. 'There are limits to the sacrifices I'm prepared to make, and I'm way past them already.'

Lenka made more coffee. She handed him his mug and sat back down beside him.

'I won't ask what you will do now, Harry – in future, I mean. It's too soon. You are welcome to stay here for a little while, but in the morning I must leave you. I am wanted elsewhere,' she added with a wry shrug.

'Of course.'

Tomorrow? He hadn't given it a moment's thought. Today had been spent living minute by minute. And right now, he didn't want the present ever to end.

'I'll let you know what I'm doing,' he said. 'I'll find a way of letting you know.'

'Thank you,' she said with a nod.

They sat in a companionable silence for a little while then, listening to Lisa snore, and thinking about snow and, in his case, wondering about one or two things.

'How did you know it was Lisa?' he asked.

'What?'

'When her picture came up on TV, how did you know it was her?'

'I wondered if that would bother you,' she said with a sad smile.

'It did, rather.'

He waited for her answer. The question suddenly seemed important again.

'I have a life, Harry, and I have a job. And Marika was a colleague, as well as a friend. Of course I knew it was Lisa.'

He suddenly felt naïve. She would have seen photos. There must be more information on file than he had assumed. He felt a bit flat, let down. She could have told him.

'Do you understand?' Lenka added. 'Some things I can't

tell you, even now.'

He nodded wearily. 'I was just surprised.'

'Don't let it come between us, Harry.'

'No, of course not.'

At least she had dispelled an awkward doubt that had been troubling him under the surface, and would almost certainly have come back to haunt him when all the excitement had died away.

'Lenka, there's something else I haven't asked you yet, something more personal. Are you alone now? I mean, do you live alone?'

She shook her head. 'I live with Stefan,' she said. 'We have been together for a little while, and things seem to be good.'

'Is he from . . . our world?'

'Definitely not, thank God!'

With a little chuckle, she added, 'He has business interests, and they take him away from home a lot. He is away at the moment, actually, which is convenient for me.'

'What does Stefan think you do for a living?'

'Oh, he knows nothing about all this. He just thinks I'm a desk-bound civil servant, and I take care not to tell him any different. For the moment, that is. Perhaps I will tell him one day, if we stay together.'

Harry nodded. 'I don't blame you. That's the best way to keep it.'

'It's not like with you and Marika.'

No.'

She was right, he thought. It wasn't. But those days had come to an end, a long time ago.

'Thanks again for all you've done, Lenka. You've been wonderful. I do know you have your own life to lead, and I've taken you away from it.'

'As I keep saying, Harry, Marika was my friend. You are my friend, too, and now so is Lisa.'

He could think of nothing worth saying to that. He just took her hand and gently squeezed.

Chapter Nineteen

'What did he say?' Murphy asked after Jackson had put the phone down.

'He wanted to know who he had with him, who else was doing the shooting.'

'What did you tell him?'

Jackson shook his head wearily. 'I told him we had no idea. It was dark. The shots were coming from inside the archway. We couldn't see who it was. He wasn't best pleased.'

'Fuck him!' Murphy said.

'You want to tell him that?'

Murphy smouldered.

'So we have new orders,' Jackson said, trying to be diplomatic.

'What – look for them?'

Jackson shook his head. 'We're running out of time. He wants us to quit pussy-footing around and go for the jugular. We're authorized to ask people where Gibson is. We can use whatever pressure is necessary.'

'That might work,' Murphy said thoughtfully. 'That's a lot better.'

'Exactly.'

'Better than riding around the city looking for him.'

'I should say so.' Jackson grinned. 'It could be all over by tomorrow night.'

'Amen to that!'

Chapter Twenty

The next morning Lenka left early, before Lisa was awake.

'Say goodbye to her for me, Harry.'

'Of course. And before you ask, I still don't know what we're going to do yet, or where we're going to go. We'll have some breakfast together, and then. . . .' He shrugged. 'Whatever we do, we'll do it together.'

'Of course. Take her far away from here, Harry. Make a fresh start.'

He smiled. 'We'll see. And you? What will you do?'

'Revert to normal. Go back to what I usually do.'

He wondered if there would be any problems for her resulting from yesterday's shenanigans, but decided not to ask. She would just have to handle them if there were, and he knew she was well capable of that. Anyway, there was nothing useful he could do, and he wasn't even going to try. His priority was Lisa.

'Take care, Harry!'

'And you.' He smiled. 'Thanks again, Lenka.'

After Lenka had left, he rooted around and found some bits and pieces for breakfast. Nothing fresh of course, but a surprisingly wide choice of things in packets and tins. Lisa, when she awoke, declared a preference for macaroni cheese of all the options available. So he had that, too. And coffee; Lisa chose orange juice. It was like being on holiday.

'Now, young lady,' he said while they ate, 'how are you this fine morning?'

She beamed him an answer and kept on eating.

Afterwards, he was content to sit back for a while and get to know his daughter all over again. For security reasons – hers – he had never seen a lot of her. It had seemed safer to keep well away. Besides, looking after a young girl didn't fit well with how he lived.

Marika – happy as she had been at the prospect, and then the reality, of parenthood – had known that too. 'We will manage,' she had declared.

And so they had, for a time. Then the roof had fallen in. Marika had been killed when a truck crushed her little car on the highway from Prague to Brno. It had probably been a simple accident, though in their line of work few believed in such things. After that, he had taken the baby to Babička, and had seen her only occasionally from that day on.

He shook his head impatiently. No point going there now. Sadly, Marika was long gone, and Lisa was a proper little going concern. He had to live in the present.

Relaxed, he watched with amusement as Lisa roamed around their refuge, exploring with eyes and fingers, and providing a running commentary on everything that came to her attention. He felt they were safe here. The world was at bay. They had food, water, heat. They could stay here forever, if needs be. Well, nearly.

'Daddy? Where are the windows? I want to see the snow.'

Ah! Perhaps the magic of their seclusion was wearing thin already. Lisa had exhausted the possibilities of their room in the nuclear shelter.

'There are no windows, Lisa. We're in a cave inside a mountain, remember?'

She took that in again and nodded. 'Can we go outside? Can I play in the snow?'

'Well. . . .'

It was then that the spell broke and he realized they couldn't actually stay here forever, after all. They had lives to lead.

'Come and talk to me, Lisa. We'll go outside in a little while.'

She sat beside him happily, and held on to him with her delicate little hands.

'Will we be together now for always,' she asked, using all her accumulated female wiles, 'like you promised?'

'Yes, of course,' he said, wondering how to make that possible – and trying to remember if he had ever actually said *for always*, or if it was a Lisa invention. Not that he minded; it was what he himself wanted too.

'Because you said – you promised – didn't you?' she persisted.

He nodded agreement. Then a solution came to him. It came with such clarity and certainty that he paused for a moment, wondering how long the idea had been gestating inside his head, or his heart.

'Would you really like to go to England?' he asked. 'Is that what you want?'

'Yes! Of course. I said so, didn't I?'

'It might be difficult. Babi wouldn't be with us, and you will have to leave your friends behind.'

She shrugged. 'I will be with you,' she said, as if that was all that really mattered.

Dear God! He thought with wonder. Just like her mother.

So they had decided. They would go to England. And once there, he resolved, they would live quiet, ordinary lives, like most people. It was possible. It could be done.

He felt the lining of his jacket and satisfied himself that the British passport he had for Lisa was there still, deep in the lining. He had always known this day might come. So he had long carried with him the one thing that Lisa would need when it did.

Briefly, he considered going just as they were, with their passports and precious little else, but he soon decided it wasn't practicable. The money he needed for their foreseeable future was in the car parked in the street near Jan Klaus's restaurant. There wasn't much else of importance in the car, but he didn't want to abandon what little there was. He would need a car at the other end, too. So they were going to have to hope it was still there; if it was, they would collect it and travel overland.

That would be safer than flying anyway. His guess was that they wouldn't get through Prague airport undetected by the various intelligence agencies that would be stationed there, and wherever they landed in the UK, someone would be waiting for them, alerted by the online scanning systems. Better to turn up at a ferry terminal, buy a ticket on the spot and slip in quietly through the backdoor, as he had done before.

Lisa was excited at the prospect. She could hardly wait to get moving. So they gathered together a few things they might need, tidied up a little and then, carefully, he switched off the lights and opened the great door that would permit them back into the outside world.

*

It was a wintry scene that confronted them. The snow was deeper than ever. They were not well equipped to deal with it, and he knew they would have to do some shopping for cold-weather gear as soon as possible. First though, they needed to get back to Malá Strana, and see if the car was still there.

Fortunately, some of the trams were running. They sheltered in a shop doorway until one they could use came along. Not many people were aboard and they soon found seats. Lisa was subdued, which was a relief. He didn't want her attracting attention.

Back in Malá Strana, the car was just as he had left it. He started it up and got the heater going full blast. Then he got to work with the shovel he had bought at a hardware store, clearing a passage through the huge ridge of snow created by passing ploughs. Half an hour later, they were on their way.

He drove around to Jan Klaus's place, intending to pick up a few things from his room there. But as soon as he entered the street, he changed his mind; a small crowd was gathered outside the restaurant, around an ambulance. He kept going, and as he drove past he saw paramedics bringing out a stretcher. They were not hurrying, which was always a bad sign. Then he saw Lenka, pushing through the throng to reach the stretcher.

A couple of blocks away he stopped the car and reached for his phone.

'Daddy?' Lisa said.

'It's all right, sweetheart. I just need to make a phone call.'

'But I saw Lenka,' she said, puzzled. 'In the street, where the ambulance was.'

'Yes, I did, too. Don't worry about it. I'm just going to make this phone call. Then we'll be on our way.'

He made the call.

'I'm busy right now,' Lenka snapped.

'I saw that, as we passed. What's going on?'

'Jan Klaus has been shot.'

'Badly hurt?'

'Dead. I have to go.'

The phone went blank. He stared at the screen for a moment. Then he slid the phone into his pocket and stared unseeingly through the windscreen. Klaus shot dead? That was something else to think about.

Fortunately, he reminded himself, he wasn't the one who had to do it.

They stopped at a big supermarket on the edge of the city and bought a few things for the journey. Then they got going again, winding their way through the outer suburbs and onto the motorway leading, via Ústí nad Labem, to the German border.

They made surprisingly good progress. Snow fell from time to time, especially on the autobahn across the high plateau of east Germany, but the authorities were well prepared to deal with it and the roads were kept passable.

Cocooned in a big quilt he had bought, Lisa would sleep from time to time and then come back to life and talk. Lord, how she talked! He didn't mind. He was glad to let her, and sometimes to listen. She seemed happy, and so was he, as they travelled towards their new life together. He wasn't going to worry about Jan Klaus, or the few possessions he had left in Jana.

It was as they rolled off the ferry in Dover that Lisa became concerned about where they were going. He hadn't thought much about that but almost instinctively he knew the answer when she asked.

'Will we go to London, Daddy?'

'Not London, no. Somewhere smaller.'

They spoke English now. He had told her that it would be best to practise the language now they were on their way to England. The last thing he wanted was someone, some observant official perhaps, becoming suspicious because Lisa was speaking a different language to him. Such little details were always a potential hazard in the life he had led for so many years.

'Where?' Lisa demanded. 'Where will we go?'

'You'll see. Somewhere you haven't heard of. We should get there late this afternoon.'

Then the conversation faltered, as Lisa became excited at seeing so many cars and trucks driving on the wrong side of the road.

Chapter Twenty-One

He drew up outside The Running Man, switched off the engine, and stretched. They were here. And nothing had happened on the way. They were out of it. Safe.

He smiled wearily, but also with relief and satisfaction. Then he turned to see how his passenger was doing. Now their motion and the engine noise had ceased, she was waking up. A head emerged from the confines of the quilt. Bleary eyes opened. A smile began to form when she saw him.

'Where are we, Daddy?'

'We're here! This is where we will stay, I hope.'

Lisa scrambled forward. 'The Running Man?' she said slowly, reading the inn sign. 'That's a funny name.'

'Isn't it? Come on! Let's see if they have a room for us.'

'Looking for a room?' said a man usually seen behind the bar, but now polishing brasses.

'That's right, George.'

'I'll just get Ellie.'

Lisa was fascinated by the décor of the reception area. She stared with intense curiosity at the fox's head, before turning to the huge salmon in a glass display case.

Harry smiled. 'This place used to be a hunting lodge.'

'In the olden days?'

'Yes, that's right.'

'Harry!'

He turned and smiled at Ellie as she bustled along the corridor from the kitchen.

'You're back!'

'Hello, Ellie!' He nodded happily. 'Yes, I'm back.'

She held out her hand. He took it, and held on for a moment longer than necessary. She seemed to want to give him a hug.

'You look . . . different, somehow,' she said, her eyes searching his face for clues. 'Tired again, but . . . happier?'

'All of that,' he agreed, letting go reluctantly of her hand.

Lisa tore herself away from the fox's head and came to stand between them, looking up at Ellie.

'Oh, my!' Ellie chuckled. 'Now, who are you? Hello, dear!'

'*Dobrý den*,' Lisa said, forgetting. 'I mean, hello.'

'My daughter, Lisa,' Harry said shyly, but proudly.

Ellie stooped to give the little girl a hug. 'How wonderful that you've come, too!'

'It was a long way,' Lisa said solemnly.

'Was it? Was it, really? Well, you're here now. And no doubt hungry and thirsty. And wanting a room with a small bed, as well as a big one?' she asked, straightening up and addressing Harry.

'If it's possible,' he agreed.

'Oh, yes. It's possible.' She smiled and added in a shy undertone, 'I hoped you would come back one day.'

'I was counting on that,' he told her gravely.

They ate supper in a corner of the bar, where there were

several other couples who had eschewed the pleasures of the empty and rather forlorn dining room. Lisa was intrigued, and tempted, by traditional bangers-and-mash. Harry had poached salmon – fresh, local salmon, Ellie told him with a gleam in her eye.

'Poached?' he queried, eyebrows raised.

'Oh, yes! The very best.'

Afterwards, Ellie brought coffee and joined them.

'Is the room all right?' she asked.

'Perfect, thank you,' Harry assured her.

'I really like my bed,' said Lisa, not to be sidelined.

'That's good!'

Later, much later, when Lisa was fast asleep and The Running Man had grown quiet and dim, Harry opened the door to a gentle tap.

Ellie smiled at him uncertainly. He reached out, took her hand and gently drew her inside. He closed the door and turned back to her. When she slipped off the coat she was wearing, he saw why she had needed it.

'You'll catch cold!' he whispered, taking her in his arms.

'Don't let me,' she murmured.

In the morning, Lisa woke before him. He surfaced to the sound of her chattering to a teddy bear she had somehow acquired. From Ellie? He kept his eyes closed for a few moments longer and felt in the empty space beside him. Ellie was gone, he realized. Of course she was. She had a hotel to run.

He sat up and glanced at his watch. Nearly 8 a.m. God! In Czech time it was 9 a.m. He couldn't remember the last time he had slept this late.

Lisa leapt onto the bed and snuggled up to him.

'You're awake bright and early,' he murmured. 'Did you sleep well?'

'Yes, thank you. I like it here. Babi would like it, too. Look!' she added. 'Ellie gave me this teddy.'

He looked and admired, and wondered when that had happened. He certainly had no recollection of it.

'I'm hungry,' Lisa announced. 'Can we have breakfast?'

'Of course we can. Let's go and see what Ellie can find for us.'

'I like her,' Lisa said thoughtfully. 'I like her a lot.'

'Me, too,' he admitted, remembering how Ellie had come to him in the night, and knowing that he had wanted that to happen since the first time he had laid eyes on her.

'I like to live in a hotel,' Lisa confided after Ellie had taken their order for breakfast. 'Will we stay here, Daddy?'

'For a while.'

He distracted her with talk of what they might do that morning. For the moment, at least, his ideas and plans didn't go any further than that.

'Did you sleep well?' Ellie asked, her eyes sparkling, when she brought them bacon and eggs.

He smiled at her. 'Eventually,' he said. 'But then I couldn't wake up.'

Ellie laughed and turned to Lisa, who had brought the teddy bear to breakfast.

'You must have been up early?' Harry said, when she looked back at him.

'Six. The usual. I'm used to it. What will you do now?'

'Look round the village, I think. I've seen next to nothing of it.'

'There isn't a lot to see, but make the most of it.' She hesitated and added, 'Will I see you . . . later?'

'Of course.'

She seemed relieved that this time he wasn't leaving immediately after breakfast.

'We'll come back for lunch.'

'Yes, do. Now I'd better get on.'

She touched the back of his hand with her fingertips. He turned his hand over and briefly pressed her fingers. She smiled and left them to it.

'Why did she do that?' Lisa asked with all the curiosity and powers of observation of a 7-year-old.

'I think Ellie likes us,' he said quietly.

'Good. I like her, too.'

It was a delight to venture outside and begin exploring the village that had given him sanctuary. It was not a very big village, but it did have a decent complement of facilities. You could do or buy most things here, he thought. There was a school too, for young children. And a playground near the river.

Lisa did some exploring, without ever going far from his side, and without her eyes ever leaving him for long. He knew, could see that, like him, she was relishing their time together. The way he felt just then, there wasn't much more that he wanted out of life.

Maybe they could stay here. For good? Why not? No one here knew him, and no one he knew was aware that he was here. Not even Babi, or Lenka.

He frowned, thinking of them, wondering if he ought to let them know. There was no pressing need, he decided. Better that no one at all knew where they were. In time, he would send Babi a postcard to let her know they were well, but not where they were. He wouldn't give away information that would be dangerous in the wrong hands.

So perhaps they could just stay here? He thought about that again. The cash from the safe house, now stuffed into the back seat of the car, would last him a long time. When it ran out – even before then – he could look for some sort of work. It didn't have to be much of a job. There was bound to be something he could do around here. Then they could rent a cottage, and Lisa could go to school. Why not?

He shrugged. He didn't know why not. There was no reason at all that he could see. Perhaps Ellie could help him find work and get settled. Ah, Ellie! He smiled softly. Ellie was another good reason to think of staying here.

Ellie came to him again that night, when The Running Man was quiet and still. Winter rain pattered gently on the window and the sodium-lit street was washed bare and shiny clean. They made love in the big bed while Lisa slept on the far side of the room, not waking. Ellie didn't suggest moving to another room. She seemed to know instinctively that he wouldn't want to be separated from Lisa. He was grateful for that, as for so much else.

They made love quietly but with great intensity. He explored her, and relished the way she responded to him. When she eventually came, she shuddered in great silent convulsions that spurred him on to complete their union with excitement and wonder.

'Don't go,' he urged afterwards. 'Stay.'

'You want me to?'

'Of course.'

She settled happily and whispered, 'I'm glad you came

back. I wondered if you really would.'

'So did I,' he admitted.

'Why did you?'

He pondered the question so long that he wondered if she had fallen asleep. How could he tell her that he had feared he wouldn't be able to return?

'It just felt right,' he said eventually. 'Something I had to do.'

She kissed his neck and slid away into sleep. He lay awake for a little while before he, too, went that way, holding her in his arms still.

The next morning it was as if they were no longer customers of the hotel. Instead, they were part of its family. People – waitresses and cooks, cleaners and receptionists – were growing used to them being there. And they cherished Lisa, little Lisa who was simply everywhere.

'She's such a lovely little thing,' Ellie said, watching as in the distance Lisa helped load a tray of dishes to be taken away to be washed. 'And she's into everything!'

Harry smiled. 'She is. You're right. I never tire of watching her.'

Ellie gazed at the little girl a bit longer. Then she turned to him. 'You said that as if you're not used to being with her?'

'I'm not,' he admitted with a shrug. 'We haven't been able to spend a lot of time together.'

Ellie could then have asked him why not. He had given her the opening. But she didn't, and he blessed her for not taking advantage of it. He chided himself for being so unguarded. It was as if his normal defences had fallen away. Yet, and yet, he didn't want to lie to Ellie or mislead her.

She didn't ask him how long he would stay either. He

was grateful for that, too. The truth was that he wasn't up to explaining about either the past or the future. This was an existential time for him. He simply wanted the moment to last.

But there were questions in Ellie's head. Inevitably. One or two leaked out in a roundabout way.

'Lisa's English is very good,' she murmured.

He agreed, but didn't add anything.

'Just occasionally she says odd words in another language. What is it?'

He hesitated, but couldn't withhold the answer. 'Czech,' he said.

Then a bit more spilled out.

'Her mother, my late wife, was killed in a road accident when Lisa was a baby.'

'Oh? I'm so sorry.'

He shrugged. 'It was a long time ago.'

'Czech,' Ellie said thoughtfully, as if that explained things.

That afternoon, he felt twinges that suggested it wouldn't always be like this. He might be in limbo at present but awkward questions were starting to push to the surface. He knew they would have to be dealt with eventually, if not quite yet.

Would they still be searching for him? That was one.

Could he really stay here indefinitely, undetected? That was another.

And what about his former colleagues? Was he really going to allow their deaths to go unexplained and unavenged?

In the end, though, it was Lisa who broke through the tranquillity of their surface life.

'Daddy, when will we see Babi?' she asked.

That brought home to him that there was still a world, a life, outside the village. And there were things he needed to do. They couldn't be neglected forever. Not really.

'I must go away for a little while,' he told Ellie.

She rolled over and stared at him.

'For a few days,' he added. 'A week maybe.'

'Will you come back?'

'Of course I will! But I can't take Lisa. Will you look after her until I get back?'

'I'd love to.' She hesitated and repeated, 'You will come back for her?'

'I'll come back for you both.'

She smiled up at him. 'You don't have to say that, Harry.'

'I mean it,' he insisted, hoping it was a promise he would be able to keep.

She studied him, the smile gone now. 'You do mean it, don't you?'

He nodded. 'Very much.'

'I don't suppose you can tell me where you're going?'

He shook his head. 'Not now, not yet. But when it's over I will.'

She sat up, saying, 'So it is dangerous? There's trouble of some sort?'

He sighed and shrugged. 'Yes, unfortunately. I must try to sort it out.'

'Back there – wherever you and Lisa came from?'

He nodded. 'Ellie, you'll have to trust me. I can't talk about it now. It's not a criminal matter, though. I can set your mind at rest on that score.'

She looked away. He could sense her weighing up his words.

'The trouble,' he added, 'is to do with my job, the work I've done for many years. That's finished now. But I still need to deal with certain issues that remain.'

'I don't understand any of this,' she said slowly. 'But I trust you. Perhaps I'm being naïve, but I do. What about afterwards, though?'

'I will come back here,' he explained patiently. 'We'll make a life together, if that's what you want. It is what we want, Lisa and I.'

'Me, too. Take care, Harry Gibson,' she said softly, leaning down to kiss him. 'And mean what you say.'

He did mean it. He just hoped he could do what he had promised.

Chapter Twenty-Two

Back in Prague, not much had changed. The temperature was a couple of degrees below freezing and snow lay all around, much of it pretty dirty and sometimes slushy on the roads. The other thing that hadn't changed, Harry acknowledged, was that he still knew next to nothing about what was going on here.

An unwelcome extra problem now was his slight uncertainty, suspicion if you like, about Lenka, and what she and her colleagues knew. More than him, that was for sure. But he had to swallow that. She had helped him. Nobody else had.

He still had his keys to Jan Klaus's place but he couldn't use them. Something had happened there, something bad. Although he had no idea what it was, he couldn't rule out the possibility that it was connected to his own recent presence there. So instead, he found accommodation in a small establishment not far away that advertised itself as a 'boutique hotel'. He had never been in one of them before, but it didn't seem much different from any other small hotel.

Late afternoon, the light fading fast, he stood near the window of his room and looked out across the rooftops of this mysterious city he had come to know so well. It was a kind of homecoming. He wasn't at peace here now – how could he be? – but the familiarity of it was in a strange way settling. Here, at least, he had few illusions and knew what to expect. He knew how things worked.

The journey had left him tired, but nervous energy was keeping him going, and he had things to do. First he phoned Babička.

'Babi?'

'Oh, Mr Harry!'

'You are well, Babi?'

'Yes, yes! Of course. How is. . . ?'

'Also well, thank you. Well and happy. I just wanted you to know that. Later, Babi, I will come to see you, but not now. Now is difficult.'

'Thank you for letting me know. I understand.'

Understand? He doubted it, he thought with a wry smile after he had switched the phone off. She was just very good, very patient, and always had been.

Next, he tapped his fingers on the window ledge for a few moments, making up his mind. Then he rang Lenka. He couldn't start distrusting her now, all because she hadn't told him she had seen a photograph of Lisa.

'I'm back,' he said. 'Can you talk?'

'Oh, hello! Not at the moment, thank you, but it is good of you to call. I'll let you know.'

He switched off and shook his head. How nice it must be to have a phone conversation that was straightforward and without danger to anyone. He wondered if that day would ever come for him.

A few minutes later, his phone vibrated and buzzed. He glanced at the screen and switched on.

'Where are you?'

He gave her his new address.

'I'll come to you when I can,' she said.

He switched off. Lenka, he had to remember, had another life, and in that life she had a job and did work for which she got paid. She needed that job. He should remember that.

It was an hour later that she arrived, tapping gently on his door. He smiled a welcome and gave her a hug.

'You got her out all right?' Lenka asked.

'Yes. She's somewhere safe now. Don't worry.'

'In England?'

He nodded.

'Thank goodness! I worried about her so much.'

'Sit down, Lenka. I was just about to make some coffee. Will you have some?'

'Thank you, yes.'

She flopped onto the bed, looking as tired as he felt. The life they led wasn't an easy one, he thought ruefully.

'Those men,' she said, sitting up. 'Jackson and Murphy, you said they were called?'

'That's right.' He emptied the sachets of coffee into two mugs and waited until the kettle switched itself off. 'What about them?'

'The car they were driving – the Jaguar?'

He nodded and poured the hot water into the mugs. 'Milk?' he asked, inspecting the sachets with suspicion.

'No, thank you.'

He sniffed and decided to have his black, as well.

'Thank you.' Lenka reached for her mug. 'It was registered with the British Embassy – CD plates, and everything.'

'Now there's a surprise,' he said with a chuckle devoid of any hint of amusement. 'Who'd have thought it?'

'Not very clever, was it?'

He shook his head. 'They must have trouble getting the staff these days. So how did they play it, when the police wanted to know what the hell was going on?'

Lenka squinted at him as she sipped her near-boiling coffee and grimaced.

'They claimed they were under attack by armed terrorists who had ambushed them. Their car had been immobilized and they were being fired on. They had to get out of the car and shoot back to defend themselves.'

'Sounds reasonable.' He shrugged. 'Did the police buy it?'

'The real police, you mean? Not entirely, no. They were concerned at bystander reports of a young girl being involved. They are investigating the possibility of Jackson and Murphy being involved in child smuggling. The Embassy, of course, is claiming that is outrageous.'

'As they would.' He nodded appreciatively. 'Anything else?'

'Not really. Some kind of talks are still going on between the Brits and the Ivans, but we're not in the loop. Perhaps you were right about the gas crisis.'

'Nothing on Unit 89?'

She shook her head. 'So what do you want to do now?'

He sat down on a chair, facing her. 'I can't just leave it, Lenka. They're probably still looking for me. Jackson and Murphy, or whoever. Eventually my luck will run out and they'll find me. And Lisa, of course. Besides, I have a duty to my colleagues. I owe it to them at least to find out what the hell has been going on.'

She nodded, and then she yawned.

'Sorry, Harry!' She hurriedly clasped a hand to her mouth. 'I need some sleep.'

'Of course you do.'

They sat in silence for a little while and sipped their coffee. He could hear nothing of the world outside. The snow must have cleared Charles Bridge of tourists. Nothing else would have done it.

'What about Jan Klaus?' he asked, a little surprised Lenka had not already brought the subject up.

She sighed and gave a shrug; despair, the message.

'He was shot, and killed. Two men came to the restaurant. They questioned him about the guests in the rooms above. Then they had him take them upstairs to see for themselves.

'The staff say that was the last they saw of Jan alive. When someone went upstairs later to look for him, they found him dead. The two men were gone.'

'No one heard a gunshot?'

She shook her head. 'Whoever killed him used a silencer.'

Harry nodded. It all made depressingly familiar sense.

'Where was the body?' he asked.

'In your room,' she said bleakly. 'From witness descriptions, the two men sounded like Jackson and Murphy.'

He grimaced. 'I'm sorry. Poor man. So they are still hunting for me?' he added.

'I am afraid so. Harry, Jan was a very old friend. You have brought a lot of trouble to this city.'

He looked at her sharply. 'Not me, babe. I 'm an innocent bystander, remember?'

She didn't reply. Instead, she got up to go. She was upset.

'Don't go, Lenka. Not like this.'

An idea had come to mind. He thought it through, and hesitated, but he had to do something and he could think of nothing better.

'I'm going to phone the embassy,' he said. 'I'm going to make contact. It's no good waiting for them to come to me. I can't hide forever.'

She stared at him. 'What do you have in mind?'

'Throwing a rock into the pool,' he said with a grim smile. 'I want to see how the ripples spread.'

To the switchboard receptionist at the British Embassy, he said, 'I have important information regarding the embassy car that was trashed in Vyšehrad a few days ago. I want to speak to someone who might be interested.'

'May I have your name, sir?'

'Not at this stage. Just find someone for me to speak to about the incident.'

'One moment, please, sir.'

He waited patiently. He could imagine the scene at the other end. People coming to the end of a long day, anxious to get home before the temperature plummeted and the weather closed in again. Then some crackpot phones when the people who matter have already left the building. Where's the duty officer?

'Can I help you?'

'One of your cars was involved in an incident the other day in Vyšehrad. A black Jaguar? I was there, and I need to speak to whoever is investigating.'

'An incident, you say?'

'An ambush,' he said, throwing caution to the wind. 'We exchanged gunfire.'

To hell with pussyfooting about. Let him pick the pips out of that one!

'Ah!'

'My name is Mr Black. I will phone again in exactly ten minutes, and announce my name to the switchboard. I expect to be put through to a competent officer then.'

He switched off.

'Interesting,' Lenka murmured. 'What is that English phrase? A bull in a china shop?'

He wasn't amused. 'Exactly. I need to make progress.'

'*We* need to make progress, Harry.'

He looked at her, wondering. 'You're still with me?'

'Of course.'

He nodded. They sat in silence then and concentrated on their coffee.

'It's Mr Black.'

'One moment, please, sir.'

A new voice took up the challenge. This was an older, more experienced – presumably more senior – person.

'Mr Black?'

'Yes.'

'I understand you have knowledge of an incident in Vyšehrad the other day?'

'I do, indeed. Are you the right person for me to be talking to?'

'Regrettably, no. The person you need to speak to is not actually here at the moment. Can we phone you back?'

He chuckled. 'I don't think so, do you?'

'Quite.'

The voice was not at all fazed, indeed was prepared for all eventualities.

'In that case,' it said now, 'I can give you a telephone number where you can reach the appropriate person. Do you have a pen handy?'

He smiled. Diplomats' games! Avoid being caught holding the parcel when the music stops. And pass the parcel on to someone you don't know, have never met, and who can never again be found or traced.

He wrote down the number and switched off the phone.

'We're getting somewhere,' he said.

'To someone you know?'

'Probably not, no. They wouldn't be that daft.'

On the other hand, he thought, why not? If they wanted to cancel his contract, why not set him up with a familiar name or face, one he thought he could trust?

'Be careful, Harry.'

He smiled and nodded.

The phone was answered immediately when he called the number he had been given.

'It's Mr Black. I believe you're expecting me?'

'Ah, yes! Mr Black. Good evening.'

It was a sharp, crisp voice, a no-nonsense, modern kind of voice. There was authority behind it, too. Not, then, one of the old brigade, Harry thought. Not a relic from gentlemen's-club land.

'I understand you have some information that may be of interest to me?'

'It's possible.'

'What kind of information?'

'I was there, at the time. I ambushed the car. That good enough for you?'

'Yes, indeed.' Short pause, then: 'Is it possible that you are the gentleman we have been seeking?'

'Seeking? Trying to eliminate more like it! I want to know why.'

He could picture the expression of concern and anguish at the other end of the line. Already things had been mentioned that normally would not be.

'Then we need to meet,' the voice said briskly. 'I can tell you now mistakes have been made. Instructions have been misinterpreted, indeed wilfully exceeded. I need to explain all this to you – and to apologize in person.'

Harry frowned. There was something about the voice, something familiar.

'Do I know you? Have we met?'

'I don't think so.'

He toyed with the idea of tossing names onto the table, and blowing trade craft out of the window. But he knew the guy would probably just switch off if he tried that.

'We can't really discuss these matters now, Mr Black. I'm sure you know why. We need to meet.'

'Where would you suggest?'

He was given an address in the Old Town. It wasn't a place he knew. But at least it wasn't in the centre of Charles Bridge at midnight, and he didn't have to carry a copy of *The Times* folded under his arm. Definitely not Old School.

'Will you go?' Lenka asked afterwards.

'I must. If I don't, how am I ever to get any answers, or have any chance of getting out of this?

'Backup would be good,' he added, looking at her.

She nodded. 'Of course. How long have we got?'

'He wants to meet at nine.' He glanced at his watch and added, 'In two hours' time.'

'I'll go now,' Lenka said, getting to her feet. 'Be careful,' she added. 'Remember this may not be what you hope.'

He sat down and switched on the television. It wasn't that he had time to kill; it was more that he needed to turn his mind to something else for a while.

A news programme was running. He watched footage of snow ploughs in the Moravian Highlands and people skiing in the Krkonoše. In Eastern Bohemia, a train was caught in an avalanche that had swept across the line. A couple of hundred people were left stranded.

It was colder, much colder, in Russia and Ukraine, where temperatures were down to -30c, and even lower in places. In Poland, too. But the common experience and suffering wasn't stopping yet another round of angry negotiations about gas prices, with Russia threatening once again to reduce supplies in the pipeline running through its neighbour, Ukraine.

Western Europe was a bit chaotic, apparently, with some major transport arteries blocked by snow or chains of accidents. In the UK it wasn't too bad. Cold for there, but nothing like most of Europe.

The main worry in the UK was the security of energy supplies, especially of gas. Once again, he heard, the country was not well placed, being at the end of the supply line and having little in the way of storage capacity. And, unlike France, the UK had turned its back on nuclear energy many years ago. Library film of wind generators on hills and in the sea suggested the main sources of alternative energy, but their contribution to the national energy supply was pitiful.

Log fires and wood-burning stoves were good, though, he thought with a wry smile. So Lisa and Ellie should be all right. The Running Man had mountains of firewood standing in the yard behind the main building. Enough to last a lifetime.

He yawned and switched off the television. Time to think about going to his meeting. Time to make sure he knew what he wanted to ask and to say. Time to find a way of putting an

end to this nonsense, and to let Lisa and himself get on with
their lives.

Chapter Twenty-Three

For once, they met face-to-face. Jackson found that better. He was tired of being the go-between. Murphy could hear it direct this time.

The boss was not in a good mood. No change there. But this time they didn't have to bear the brunt of his displeasure.

'This guy – Klaus – told you nothing?'

'I wouldn't say that. He admitted Gibson had been there. He just didn't tell us where he is now. Couldn't, I mean. He didn't know.'

'So we popped him,' Murphy contributed. 'No point leaving him to tell the world about us.'

Jackson winced as he saw the way the boss looked at Murphy.

'There was a risk,' Jackson intervened. 'We didn't want him identifying us.'

The boss was happier with that. A civilized man, the boss.

'Quite so,' he said.

Jackson hurried on. 'So we still don't know where he is. We don't even know if he's in the country.'

The boss frowned. 'Time is running out, gentlemen. We need to find him, and fast. Otherwise, all this will have been for nothing. We'll have nothing to show for our labours.'

Murphy seemed about make a contribution. Jackson silenced him with a fierce glare.

'You know where to go next, don't you?' the boss said. 'There is at least one person who must have a very good idea where he is.'

Jackson nodded. 'She'll know where they both are.'

'Right, gentlemen,' the boss said, getting to his feet. 'I'll leave it to you.'

They sat still for a few moments after he had left the room. Jackson listened hard, but couldn't hear a whisper as the man made his exit.

'Gentlemen?' Murphy murmured. 'Is that what we are now?'

Jackson grinned. 'We'd better get to work,' he said. 'Justify his good opinion of us.'

'It's nice to have something to do,' Murphy countered. 'Makes it all seem worthwhile.'

Jackson relaxed. His partner was in a good mood. When they got their hands on the money, he would be in an even better mood.

Chapter Twenty-Four

Lenka phoned.

'I don't like the location, Harry.'

'What's wrong with it?'

'Too many ways in and out. You would be very vulnerable. I don't think you should go. There are safer places to meet than that.'

He thought quickly. It was unfortunate, but he trusted Lenka's judgement.

'I still need to know who this guy is,' he pointed out.

'I can go. They don't know me.'

That made sense. Let Lenka see who turned up. Find out who he was dealing with.

'OK. But be careful!'

He stayed where he was. There was time to kill now. So he switched the television back on, just in time to catch the end of yet another news bulletin dealing with weather-induced catastrophe. Rather, with the political fallout.

Now Germany was displaying concern with the situation in Ukraine. There must be no repeat, Chancellor Merkel warned, of the breakdown in relations that several years ago had led to unnecessary deaths in Romania, Slovakia and elsewhere. If the security of Russian gas supplies could not be guaranteed, then purchasing countries would need to think again about where they went for their supplies, and what kind of energy to use.

He switched off. The same old thing; Russia had the gas, the rest of Europe wanted it badly. But it was hard to see what the point was of negotiations in Prague between Russia and the UK. Britain was a European sideshow, even if it did like to think of itself as a top-table member.

He shook his head and glanced at his watch. He was on edge. Lenka must be there now. He hoped she would appear to be just another diner in the restaurant. There was no reason for anyone to single her out if she was careful. She would be careful, of course, but still it was worrying.

She returned just after ten.

'There were three of them,' she said tersely. 'Jackson, Murphy and, presumably, your contact.'

'Christ! Jackson and Murphy again? Where were they?'

'The contact came inside, sat down and ordered a drink. The other two stayed outside in a car.'

He nodded and swore softly. It was no different, then. They were still trying to eliminate him. Nothing had changed. How could he ever have thought it might have?

Lenka started fiddling with her phone. He paced up and down the room, working out what to do next.

'The meetings at the embassy are still going on,' Lenka said, studying her phone. 'The Brits and the Russians.'

He nodded but he didn't care. It was nothing to do with him now. He had other things on his mind.

'Oh, that's interesting!'

He looked round.

'I took a photo of your contact in the restaurant. I didn't recognize him but I sent it to a colleague. He says the man has just entered the British Embassy.'

She looked up.

He shrugged. 'We knew he was connected there.'

'Yes, but how?'

A potential answer came to him. 'Possibly through the gas deal. He has to be able to tell the Russians that Unit 89 has been totally eliminated before they agree to send more gas – by tanker, presumably.'

'You really think that?'

'I do. The UK is desperate. The cold weather will be using up all the reserves and, like we said before, the Russians drive a hard bargain. They'll want something, as well as money, in return – all sorts of things, probably.'

'And the scalps of you and the rest of your unit might be one of them?'

'It's a reasonable proposition. In a national emergency, individuals become expendable, especially people who don't officially exist anyway.'

Lenka shrugged again and yawned. 'It's possible, I suppose.'

'Damn right it is!'

He picked up the phone and rang the number again.

'It's Mr Black.'

'Ah! Where were you, Mr Black? You didn't come.'

'You weren't alone. You brought to the meeting the very people who have been trying to kill me. Not good enough, I'm afraid.'

'Perhaps we can make another arrangement?'

No attempt to deny anything.

'Perhaps we can. This time I will tell you where we meet. And, boy, you'd better come alone!'

According to tradecraft convention, a meeting like this had to be somewhere safe and secure. A quiet venue, in other words, where threats could be spotted and evaded.

That was the theory. But, instead, Harry nominated a small café in the Lucerne complex just off Wenceslas Square. It was in the heart of a maze of internal shopping arcades built a century ago by the late President Havel's family, Havel himself in his years as a dissident being no stranger to subterfuge, clandestine meetings and the need for avenues of escape.

'I know it well,' Harry said after he had ended the phone call. 'There are plenty of ways out of it if things go badly.'

Lenka smiled. 'You could even escape from the balcony where Havel showed Dubček to the crowds in Wenceslas Square, back in 1989.'

'Wouldn't that be something?'

All that was back then, when Czechoslovakia still existed, Communists governed and the Soviet Union called the shots.

'I will bring a colleague,' Lenka added, 'and we'll watch the approaches to the café. We don't want your friends Jackson and Murphy turning up again uninvited.'

He nodded. 'Thanks. If things don't go well, I'll make my exit through the kitchen and out into the music shop in the next arcade.'

'It sounds like you've done that before?'

'Once or twice,' he admitted with a smile.

Simon Mayhew sat waiting for him.

Harry was astonished. Suppressing his surprise, he

glanced around before making his approach. Mayhew seemed to be alone.

'I wasn't expecting you to be here,' he said as he sat down.

'Get used to it. I'm here.'

Harry caught the eye of a waiter, who promptly came over. He ordered a beer and glanced at Mayhew, who shook his head and pointed to his coffee cup.

Once the waiter had left them, Mayhew said, 'So what do you want, Gibson? You've caused us enough trouble already.'

The niceties were over, it seemed. Harry shook his head in disbelief, and with irritation. 'And you such a busy man?' he suggested.

Mayhew was not amused. 'We are short-handed at present, as it happens. Otherwise it certainly wouldn't be me sitting here. Now, what do you want?'

He had wondered about that, about why Mayhew had turned up. Budget cuts must be biting deep.

'All hands on deck when it comes to talking to the Russians, eh? I don't blame you.'

Mayhew didn't give anything away. He simply stared, his face without expression.

'You and I met once before,' Harry reminded him. 'Many years ago.'

'I remember.'

'I thought then you were an arrogant, unpleasant bastard. Nothing's happened to change my mind.'

The waiter arrived with the beer.

Mayhew waited until he had departed. Then he leaned forward and said, 'Don't waste my time. Our country is in difficulties, and I have a lot to do without you creating more trouble.'

'Me, creating trouble?' Harry shook his head and sighed

with frustration. 'All I want to know is why you've been trying to kill me, and when it will stop. That straightforward enough for you?'

There was a long silence before Mayhew responded. 'Are you quite well, Gibson?'

'Well enough, thank you. What about my questions?'

'Absolute rubbish, as you well know.'

Mayhew glanced at his watch and shuffled in his seat, about to stand up.

'Then why did I mount the attack on the car?'

'So it was you?'

He nodded.

'Look, Gibson. What do you want?'

'I've told you. I want to know why you've been trying to kill me.'

'That's fantasy, total fantasy. What on earth is wrong with you?' Mayhew asked, staring at him hard.

'Fantasy, is it? Then tell me what happened to the rest of Unit 89 – and to Callerton, the man who created it in the first place. Tell me that!'

'The Callerton part is easy. I happen to know that Callerton is living happily in retirement in the Lake District.'

Harry shook his head impatiently. 'Not when I saw him last, he wasn't. Someone had just shot him. Half his head had been blown off.'

'Rubbish!'

'Look, I'm sick and tired of all this. I've had enough. It goes against my instincts but I'm prepared to make a deal with you. I won't go public if you call off the dogs.'

'Dogs? There aren't any!'

Harry shook his head impatiently and pressed on. 'I know you're trying to do a gas deal with the Russians. The country needs energy, and it's difficult for you. I understand that. But sacrificing your own people in order to achieve a deal with the Russians is going too far. What I want. . . .'

Mayhew held up a hand to stop him. 'I realize,' he said in a softer tone, 'that you must have been under a lot of strain. I can understand that. It's a lonely job, out here. You need help. Take extended leave, and we'll arrange some for you. But we are meeting now because you attacked an Embassy car. Remember? I came here tonight to find out why.'

'Because the people in it had kidnapped my daughter.'

'Nonsense!'

Mayhew shook his head. He seemed genuinely exasperated.

'It's true,' Harry insisted doggedly. 'The men driving it, Jackson and Murphy, have been pursuing me for a couple of weeks – from Prague to Orkney, and back again.

'They kidnapped my daughter to bring me out in the open. She was in the car at the time I stopped it. I rescued her. Didn't you see any of that in the news? They took her from her grandmother's house, here in Prague, and set up a meeting with me that wasn't going to end well for either of us. I pre-empted them, and rescued my daughter. Now I want to bring all this to an end. So how about it?'

The fingers of Mayhew's left hand had begun to tap out a fast rhythm on the tabletop. Harry watched them, and waited.

'Who did you say was driving the car?'

'Jackson and Murphy, two cleaners. Sorry. The atmosphere where you live may be too rarefied for you to be aware of such creatures.'

Mayhew shook his head impatiently. 'My information is that the car was in the hands of someone else, someone far more important than the likes of Jackson and Murphy.'

'Who?'

Mayhew waved the question aside. He wasn't prepared to say.

'Then you'd better do some checking,' Harry said grimly, 'because I'm telling you now you've got it wrong. If you don't believe me, check with the Prague police.'

He could tell that something he had said had got Mayhew thinking. The mood of the meeting had changed.

'I'm a busy man, Gibson. We're all busy. The UK needs more Russian gas, and you're right in thinking there are negotiations going on at the moment about that. But that's nothing to do with me. I'm here for another reason. And I'm the one talking to you now because the person who ought to have met you is not available.'

'Oh? And who might that be?'

'None of your business.'

Harry shook his head wearily. 'Well, find time to check what's been going on, Mayhew, and do it yourself. You're from the UK, from outside. Things are not right here, in Prague. So check the facts, and then tell me I'm wrong.'

'If you think. . . .'

'My mobile will be switched off. I'm taking no chances. But I'll call you in the morning.

'I'm telling you now, though, that if this vendetta doesn't stop I'm going public with what's been happening, and with what I know. I'll disclose everything, and I'll do it where it will do most damage.'

'Don't threaten me, Gibson.'

'Just do it,' Harry said grimly. 'I mean what I say.'

Chapter Twenty-Five

He sensed a difference when he phoned Mayhew the next morning, and he guessed the man had done some investigating.

'Meet me this morning at ten,' Mayhew said crisply. 'The same place?'

'I'll be there.'

He switched off the phone, looked at Lenka and shrugged. 'He wants to meet again. I think he's discovered something.'

'Let's hope so – and let's hope it makes a difference.' She yawned and added, 'I'll come with you.'

'Are you sure?'

She nodded.

'What about Stefan?'

'Absence makes the heart grow fonder, doesn't it?' she said with a wry smile. 'He's not here at the moment.'

He grinned and turned away to get ready.

Mayhew took on a different tone at the meeting, treating Harry like a human being and even a valued colleague instead of a deranged alien. He looked tired as well, as if he had been up all night.

'I've done some checking,' he announced as soon as their

coffee had been delivered. 'It's not been easy overnight. And, as you know, this isn't my patch. But what you told me seems to stand up.'

Harry nodded and took a sip of coffee. 'So what have you discovered?'

Mayhew frowned, as if to discourage questions. Then he sighed. 'Sadly, Callerton is dead, as you told me. He was murdered. And some of the other things you told me I have also been able to corroborate.'

'Good.'

'Good?'

'Don't get me wrong,' Harry said with a grimace. 'I liked Callerton. I liked him a lot. I also had great respect for him.'

Mayhew nodded. 'He thought well of you, too. He made that clear in his appraisals.'

'What else have you learned?'

'Another body was found at the murder scene. Initially, the working hypothesis was that you had shot them both.

'Then it was found that the bullets had come from different guns, and that the gun found at the scene was the one used to kill Callerton. It had on it the prints of the dead man.

'After that, other things fell into place, all leading to the conclusion that the man who had murdered Callerton had himself then been killed by a third party.'

Mayhew gave him a keen look and added, 'You got there too late, I take it?'

'Just. A few minutes might have made a difference.' Harry shrugged and added, 'The killer was still in the house, waiting for me. Was he one of yours?'

'Well . . . let's just say he was known to us.'

Yes, let's! Harry thought. Then he reminded himself to treat what Mayhew was telling him with caution and suspicion. Just because he wanted him to have changed sides didn't mean that he actually had.

'What about Unit 89?'

Mayhew sighed. 'I've checked back with London. There is growing concern there. They say they can't make contact. Probably nothing, they say, but. . . .'

'That's because Landis is dead, and he was the contact point.'

'So I understand.'

An influx of new customers disrupted their conversation for a minute or two. Americans. They were ebullient, happy and enchanted by this quaint café they had stumbled upon so unexpectedly.

Mayhew was distracted, a man not comfortable amongst tourists. 'This really is a strange place, isn't it?' he said.

Harry smiled. 'I like it.'

'How did you find it?'

'I've been in Prague a long time.'

'Yes, of course you have. As long as anyone, haven't you?'

'Just about.'

'Do you know George Mason?'

He shook his head. 'Not really. I met him briefly a couple of times after he took over from Callerton. Since then, not at all.'

'But you knew he was moved here, to be station chief?'

'No. I hadn't heard that. When?'

'Fairly recently. You haven't had contact since he arrived?'

Harry shook his head. 'Landis was the one who had contact with the embassy. Maybe that was one of the things he was going to tell us at the meeting he had called.'

'Possibly.' Mayhew frowned. 'Well, from what I can gather, in the very limited time I have had to check all this, we now have a rogue senior officer here in Prague.'

Harry held his breath, stunned. 'Not Mason?'

'Exactly.' Mayhew nodded. 'And now he's missing.'

'And he initiated all this?'

'It looks very much like it.'

'Well, he's not the only one involved,' Harry said bitterly. 'I know that much.'

'You're right. Jackson and Murphy, obviously, are involved. And Mason's assistant, Grant. He's the person you were supposed to meet last night, by the way.

'Otherwise, I don't know at the moment. But there might well be others implicated, including some back at home. Mason's successor, for one. He's an old buddy of his. So there are things to check when I get back there. Frankly, it's a bit of a dog's breakfast.'

Harry shook his head. The enormity of it! Was this story credible? He stirred his coffee unnecessarily, avoiding Mayhew's eyes. Could he believe what he was hearing?

'Why?' he said eventually. 'Do you know?'

'I would only be guessing at this stage.'

'Then, guess. Humour me.'

Mayhew sighed. 'Callerton trusted you,' he said obliquely.

Harry nodded. 'Over the years I had given him good reason.'

'So I'm going to trust you, as well. You've earned it.'

'Nice of you to say so!'

Mayhew forced a thin smile. 'Don't be sarcastic with me, Harry. We need each other.'

Oh? Harry now, was it?

'Well, Simon, I've done all right so far on my own.'

'But you've hit a dead end now, haven't you?'

'Just about,' he admitted.

'OK. Try this. Mason was disenchanted, aggrieved and disappointed. You can put those words in any order you like. He wanted the job I was given. Instead, after my appointment, he was sent here. He believed here, Prague, was Nowhere Land, yesterday's front line but no longer a place to win advancement and wield influence.

'In that, he wasn't entirely wrong. Unit 89, for example, was important when Callerton set it up, but it isn't now. The Cold War, and the immediate aftermath, is ancient history. We – the service, that is – have quite different priorities now, and our manpower deployments have had to respond to that shift of focus.'

'The Arabists in the Foreign Office must be delighted.'

Mayhew gave a thin smile. 'You're not wrong. Anyway, as the new broom, I was required to help bring about these changes. My recommendation was that we reduce our commitment in central Europe and wind up organizations like your own Unit 89. To be frank, I don't know what you've been doing in recent years, and whatever it was, we don't really need it any more.'

Harry gave a rueful smile. 'I've been thinking the same thing myself for a while. But here we are still, and old habits die hard.'

Mayhew nodded. 'Anyway, that's the background.'

'So not only had Mason not got the job he wanted,' Harry reflected, 'but the one he did get was about to be chopped, and himself made redundant. I would guess that at that point he was totally pissed off, and decided to look to his own interests. Right?'

'What he thought were his own interests,' Mayhew said wearily.

'Then what?'

'Well, contrary to what you suspected, HMG has not done – and is not going to do – a shady deal with the Russians in exchange for promises of gas. I can assure you of that. However. . . .'

Mayhew paused, stared hard and added, 'However – as you want me to brainstorm – I believe George Mason very well might have done some sort of deal on his own behalf with parties unknown. I've no idea what is involved, but something has been going on. And that's why I'm here, to get to the bottom of it.'

'So you didn't come to be part of the discussions going on at the embassy about gas?'

Mayhew shook his head. 'I came because of the shenanigans at Vyšehrad, and because Mason was missing. I came to stop confusion and embarrassment becoming a crisis.

'Just for the record,' he added, 'there are no discussions going on at the embassy about gas. The UK does have problems in that area but the need is for the new pipelines under construction to be completed, not for a new gas contract with the Russians.

'The discussions going on at the embassy – involving certain Russian players, admittedly – are about our missing station chief. We had hoped our Russian counterparts might be able to shed light on that. Since I've been here, of course, I've learned that the problem is different from what I initially thought, and a lot more serious.' He winced. 'Unfortunately, it looks as though whatever deal Mason made required him to wipe Unit 89 off the map.'

It had begun to sound plausible to Harry. He wasn't sure he could take everything Mayhew had said at face value, but overall it made sense.

He shrugged and said bleakly, 'Three good men in my unit

were murdered. Three colleagues. Callerton, as well. If you're right, Mason has a hell of a lot to answer for.'

Mayhew nodded. 'It's a bad situation. I've told you what I know, and what I guess. At the moment I have nothing to add.'

'So what are you going to do about it?'

'Not a lot.' Mayhew sighed. 'There's not a lot I can do officially. The Czech Republic is a friendly and loyal ally, but it is also a country with a weak coalition government and a high regard for its own sovereignty. We do not want to embarrass our Czech friends, still less destabilize their government. We must tread carefully.'

Harry shook his head impatiently and pushed back in his chair.

'Hear me out!' Mayhew said crisply. 'I've told you the official position. Officially, we will proceed carefully. Unofficially, we will bring in search teams to look for Mason. Eventually, he will surface. God knows where, though.'

'Nice,' Harry said. It was hard not to sound sceptical.

'Be that as it may,' Mayhew continued unperturbed, 'none of this is much practical help to you personally. You need to be very careful, Harry. You remain at risk and, to be frank, there's not a lot I can do for you. Here, I can do virtually nothing. Back in the UK, there are things we could do – a new identity, and so on, if you wanted that?'

Harry shook his head. If he was to have a new identity, he would arrange it himself, not leave it to people he no longer trusted.

'Effectively,' Mayhew continued, with no attempt to sugar the pill, 'I'm sorry to say that you're on your own for the time being. Understood?'

Harry grinned. 'I've known that for a couple of weeks!'

'Good. We'll get to the bottom of it eventually, but in the meantime look after yourself.'

Mayhew pulled his sleeve up to check his watch. 'I must go. Anything else before I do?'

Harry shook his head. 'I've got the picture.' He hesitated a moment and then added, 'I appreciate your being frank with me.'

'I couldn't very well do anything else, in the circumstances. Take care, Harry. And if there is anything further, you can always contact me via the phone number you have.'

He stayed where he was when Mayhew left. He waited until Lenka joined him. Then he ordered more coffee.

'Has he gone?'

Lenka nodded. 'He went into Wenceslas Square and took the metro. He was alone. What did he say to you?'

Harry sighed. 'That I'm on my own, basically. I have to look after myself. A rogue senior officer is behind all this, and they don't know where he is right now. He's gone missing.'

'Who is that?'

'George Mason. Know him?'

Lenka shook her head.

'Well, Mayhew came to look for him, and to find out what's been going on here. He says the discussions at the embassy with the Russians are all about that, Mason's disappearance. Nothing to do with talks about gas supplies.'

Lenka frowned. 'Do you believe him?'

'I'm not sure, but I think I do. I believe he was levelling with me. The trouble is,' he added, 'I'm still at risk. Mayhew thinks Mason won't have given up hunting me.'

'Why?'

He grimaced. 'Who knows?'

'So what are you going to do?'

Harry smiled. 'That's easy. I'm going to go after him, and hope I get him before he gets me! '

Chapter Twenty-Six

In a way, the heat was off. After the meetings with Mayhew, Harry knew he didn't have the whole of Her Majesty's Government on his trail. It was just Mason, his two side-kicks, Jackson and Murphy, and a few other helpers he didn't know about. That made it seem a lot better, the odds more manageable.

He didn't know Mason. There had been a brief couple of meetings at which next to nothing was said. Just: *Carry on the good work*, basically. At the time, he had thought Callerton would prove a tough act for the new man to follow, but he hadn't thought much else. Reporting arrangements had changed after that, but not much else was different.

Then, it seemed, Mason had been moved to Prague anyway, and whoever had taken over his job in London had helped him. Landis must have discovered some of this, but he had been murdered before he could pass it on.

And now? He sighed. Now he wasn't sure what to do. He accepted Mayhew's judgement that Mason would continue trying to hunt him down, and his instinct said to go on the front foot. But if he went hunting himself, what chance would he have? The Czech Republic was not a big country, but it was big enough. And Mason could be anywhere.

On his own, with time to reflect, Harry reminded himself that it might be a mistake to assume that everything Mayhew had told him was true. Or any of it. Mayhew was a professional, a high-ranking one at that. His priority would be getting the job done, whatever the job was, and whatever it took. So it would be sensible to do some checking.

Kuznetsov liked to take morning coffee in a small restaurant just off Old Town Square. He was there, as usual, when Harry entered and sat down to order a coffee.

If Kuznetsov was surprised, he didn't show it. He didn't even glance in Harry's direction. He remained intent on a newspaper he was studying. But Harry was confident that he would have been noticed. Now Kuznetsov would be wondering why Harry had exposed himself like this, and what to do about it. It was an unusual situation.

Twenty minutes later, Harry was in the back half of a joined-up pair of trams heading towards Holešovice. Kuznetsov was somewhere in the front half; no contact had been made. Later, Harry was thinking, he might take the opportunity to visit Babička. He might as well, while he was in the vicinity.

Kuznetsov's destination, it turned out, was the Trade Fair Palace, housing the National Gallery's Collection of Modern Art. It was a vast, spacious, modernist building erected in the 1920s as a trade exhibition hall that only in more recent times had found its true vocation as an art gallery.

Kuznetsov stood rapt in thought on the third floor, studying a creature that had emerged from the imagination of a sculptor who worked in scrap metal. Harry joined him.

'Good morning, Mr Gibson. Nice to see you again. I have been missing you. I thought you must have lost interest in me.'

'Never! You are one of my special people. It's just that I have been busy.'

Kuznetsov smiled and moved to another exhibit. 'This!' he said, clasping his hands together in adulation. 'This, I understand. It is a bird, I believe, a Czech bird of some sort.'

'Or a bad dream, a nightmare?'

'Perhaps,' Kuznetsov said with a chuckle.

They had never spoken before, but Kuznetsov was turning out to be exactly as Harry had long thought him to be. It was like meeting an old friend, an imaginary pal.

'It is not us,' Kuznetsov said quietly. 'Whatever you think, I can assure you of that.'

'Then who is it?'

'Your Mr Mason is at the centre of it, here in Prague. But he is only the puppet. Someone else pulls the strings.'

'And that is?'

'Someone in London, not Moscow,' Kuznetsov said, smiling. 'London,' he emphasized. 'There is no grand conspiracy, Harry. Merely personal ambition.'

'You seem to know a lot about it.'

'Of course.' Kuznetsov inclined his head in a gesture of acknowledgement. 'We are good at this game, as you know.'

And it was true, Harry thought ruefully. He and his colleagues had been a handful of amateurs, dilettantes, by comparison.

'Mason, then?' he said.

'Yes. He has done a deal.'

'With?'

'People in London.'

'Do you know why?'

Kuznetsov rubbed finger and thumb together. 'These people are Russians – oligarchs, as they are called. They have much money, and they have offered Mason a share in a new gas field in eastern Siberia. It will be very lucrative eventually.'

So Callerton had known, or guessed, Harry thought suddenly, remembering the newspaper headline he had circled. Trust Cally!

'Do they have names, these oligarchs?'

'The principal is a man called Kurst. You may have heard of him?'

Harry shook his head.

'You will, in time. He is believed to have political ambitions, which is why Moscow would like him back, why he lives in London and why he protects himself.'

'What does he want from Mason?'

'We Russians are chess players,' Kuznetsov said with a smile. 'You of all people should know that, Harry. Who knows what the oligarchs want? Something now, something in future. Even if it is nothing now,' he added with a shrug, 'the time may come when a man who knows so much about Western intelligence will be very valuable. It is just a pity that the oligarchs thought of this before we did!'

Harry frowned with thought. 'You are sure of this?'

Kuznetsov nodded. 'The rest of your team – your Unit 89 – was killed. Yes?'

It was Harry's turn to nod. He was astonished by how much the man knew.

'The reason,' Kuznetsov continued, 'is that one of your colleagues had discovered this. The man called Landis? He was about to tell the rest of you and, presumably, London. Mason had to stop that happening. If he was discredited, his value to Kurst would be at an end, and their deal would lapse.'

So there it was, in the proverbial nutshell. Kuznetsov had

confirmed what Mayhew had told him, and then in a few words had added a whole lot more. Mystery solved. But the enormity of it almost took his breath away.

'Jesus Christ, Yuri!' Harry murmured, shocked. 'Why are you telling me all this?'

Kuznetsov smiled his enigmatic smile. 'Maybe I am tired, Harry. Maybe I, too, would like to live in London?'

Harry shook his head. 'We're all wasting our time, aren't we?' he said despairingly.

'Now, perhaps,' Kuznetsov said. He shrugged. 'The world is changing, Harry. And we must change with it.'

Chapter Twenty-Seven

Back at his hotel, he had plenty of time to mull things over. Lenka was not with him. She had said she had things to do, which he could well believe. Whether they were domestic or work things, he didn't know, but he was sure there would be plenty of them by now. Lenka had been giving him a lot of her time. She would need to catch up.

Besides, there were things about Lenka that troubled him. He needed to think about them, and perhaps get them into perspective. How much she had known all along, for example. He knew she hadn't told him everything. That still bothered him.

He also needed to talk to her about George Mason. Surely her department had some idea of where and how he lived, even if she didn't herself?

He took a tram out to Strašnická again. It was early evening by then. People were making their way home as usual. Now the weather had eased, the city was returning to normal. The main roads had been cleared of snow and abandoned vehicles, and people were back in their routines. At the stop nearest to Lenka's apartment block, there was quite a scurry as commuters flooded across the road, desperate to get home before anything else happened that day.

Harry watched them with a little envy. His own life was not like that, and never really had been. His world was no respecter of the clock. Feast or famine had been his work experience for many years, and with feast came urgency and pressure. Clock watching couldn't happen then.

He glanced at his watch; just before 7 p.m. Was he too early or too late? He had no idea how Lenka lived, or how she accommodated the clock. The assumption that she lived as he had always lived could be well wide of the mark. She was office-based; he never had been.

Her phone rang for an unusually long time before it was answered, making him think she must be out. He took it away from his ear and studied the screen, checking the number he had called. It was then it was picked up and he heard a babble of Czech commentary in a woman's voice he didn't recognize.

'Lenka, please,' he said cautiously.

After a long pause, the familiar voice came on the line. He relaxed.

'It's me, Lenka.'

'Ah! Is everything all right?'

'Yes. Nothing's changed. Are you busy?'

'What do you think? That was my mother who picked up the phone.'

He smiled. Not exactly a put-down, but close enough. Served him right.

'I'm sorry about this, Lenka. I should have called before I came. But I'm here now. Can you spare me half an hour?'

'You're here? What do you mean?'

Definitely not in friendly mode, he thought with a wince.

'I've just got off the tram, at your stop.'

'Stay there. I'll be with you in a few minutes. Better,' she added, 'there's a small bar about fifty metres away. I'll see you in there.'

He switched off and put the phone away. It sounded like he had caught her at a bad moment; she and her mother having a domestic, perhaps? That might explain why she had not invited him inside. Life was difficult enough.

To make amends for his intrusion, he turned into a little flower shop next door to the bar Lenka had designated. It was packed. People queued in that tiny space like proverbial sardines, shoulder to shoulder, arm to arm, and shuffled forward when they could. Others came into the shop behind him, preventing him leaving even if he had changed his mind. The only possibility was to reach the counter, make a purchase, and then leave by an exit behind the counter.

It was unbelievable, he mused, how many people must be living with ecstatic love or a weighty sense of duty – or a guilty conscience, like himself.

It was while he was ordering a single, special, red rose that he saw a man pause at the window and glance into the shop for a moment. He was stunned. The woman serving him had to bark out a repeat demand for his payment. There was muttering around him at the delay. Hurriedly, he thrust a hundred-crown note into the woman's hand and pushed his way out of the back of the shop.

The man was gone, disappeared, swept up in the human tide rolling onto and off a convoy of trams, and to and from the many nearby blocks of flats. Frantically, he scanned the crowds as he walked quickly about the immediate area. But it was no good. The man had vanished.

He swore softly to himself, anger and frustration replacing shock. He had no doubts about who he had just seen so fleetingly, and so improbably. The man had been George Mason. He had a good memory for faces, and he was sure of it. Quite certain.

He gave up and made his way back to the bar, where he found Lenka waiting for him. She looked up anxiously.

'Sorry,' he said. 'Something came up.'

'I thought you had got lost, or perhaps been kidnapped.'

He handed her the rose wrapped in tissue wrapper. 'For you, Lenka. I am sorry for this intrusion.'

She smiled and shook her head. 'Thank you, Harry. It is beautiful.'

He was undecided about telling her what he had seen. She might think him paranoid. Well, she knew that. He was. They all were. It went with the territory. You didn't survive if you were not at least a little bit paranoid in this business.

But ought she to be told anyway? The reason Mason might be in the vicinity – and it definitely had been Mason – might have something to do with her. She could be in danger.

He remained undecided.

There was an alternative possible explanation for Mason's presence in the area, but he really didn't want to consider that. He did have some uncertainties about Lenka, and how much she knew, but he couldn't let himself start wondering if Mason had come here to see her. Not after all she had done for him.

Anyway, perhaps he was mistaken, and it hadn't been Mason, after all.

'You look worried, Harry?'

He sighed and told her what he had seen, or what he thought he had seen.

She shrugged. 'You were mistaken, I think. He is on your

mind so much that by now you will be seeing him everywhere you look. It is only natural.'

He smiled tentatively. 'Probably. But you should take care, just the same.'

'Don't worry about me. I always take care. If I don't think of it myself, my mother scolds me until I do.

'Now, why did you want to see me?'

'Actually,' he said, 'it was about George Mason. I was wondering if there was anything you could tell me about him.'

'About George Mason?' She stared at him and shook her head. 'Harry, for God's sake! What did I just tell you? Go and get me a drink!' she added, starting to laugh.

They didn't get any further. Lenka didn't really know anything about George Mason. Someone in her department might, but she didn't.

'You couldn't find out where he lives, I suppose?'

She shrugged. 'Perhaps someone knows. But probably he is not important enough – or dangerous enough – for us to have taken such an interest.'

Until now, he thought. For me, at least.

'By the way,' Lenka said, changing the subject with a happy smile, 'I hope I will be able to introduce you to Stefan soon. I think he will be home again in the very near future.'

'That's good. I would like to meet him.'

Still smiling, she added, 'I am always happy when Stefan is here.'

He smiled back. 'I am glad for you, Lenka. You deserve someone special in your life.'

He was genuinely happy for her. Relationships had never been easy for her to make, and Lenka had always struck him as someone destined for life as a single person. It was good to know that things might be looking different.

'Will you allow me to buy you a drink?' she asked.

He shook his head. 'No thanks, Lenka. I must be getting back. Besides, your mother will complain if you go home smelling of booze.'

'Oh, her!' Lenka waved a careless hand. 'She is in a bad mood anyway. She always is when Stefan comes home.'

'Perhaps she thinks he will steal you away from her?'

Lenka laughed. He was pleased to see it, and they parted on a happy note.

While he was waiting for the tram to take him back to the city centre, his phone buzzed with a text message. He glanced at it with surprise. Ellie?

Please phone me! the message said.

What now? Only in emergencies, he had told her. Lisa? His heart began to race.

His tram arrived. He let it go and walked away from the platform, concentrating on the phone.

'Ellie? It's Harry.'

'Oh, thank goodness! How are you?'

'Fine, thanks. What's wrong?'

'Nothing! Don't worry.'

He felt his anxiety collapsing like a wet paper bag.

'Ellie, I was worried by your message. Are you sure things are all right?'

'Yes, yes. Don't worry. It's just that there's something I wanted you to know.'

'What's that?'

'But Lisa is fine. She's perfectly well.'

'And you, too?'

'Yes. Me, too. We both are very well.'

He chuckled with relief. 'So what is it, Ellie? What couldn't wait?'

'Well, I wanted to hear your voice, of course. I wanted to know you were all right. To be honest, Harry, I'm not sure about this, about what I've got myself into with you.'

He grimaced. 'There's nothing to worry about, Ellie. Anyway, it will be over soon.'

'Yes, but it's difficult for me.'

He was reminded then that he was asking an awful lot of her. 'Look, Ellie. . . .'

'There was something,' she said quickly, cutting him off. 'Lisa made a phone call.'

'Oh?'

'To the Czech Republic, to her grandmother. I thought you should know.'

'How did she do that?' he asked with astonishment.

'It's pretty simple, really. You pick up a telephone. . . .'

'Did she get through?'

'Apparently.'

'But. . . . But how did she know the number?'

'It's no good asking me. She just did. Anyway, I thought you should know.'

'You were right. Thanks. Tell her not to do it again, will you?'

Little more was said. It hadn't been an easy call, and it didn't end terribly well. He knew why. All this must be pretty inexplicable to someone like Ellie, with a life so far removed from the one he had lived for so long.

He looked around. He was the only person there now, and he was standing on the concrete platform, out in the open. The next tram couldn't come quickly enough.

While he waited, he thought about Lisa's phone call. He

didn't know how she had managed it – an overseas call, as well. Ellie had been right to tell him. But it was something else for him to worry about. The call had broken the seal around Lisa's whereabouts. Hopefully, no harm had been done, but he didn't want it to happen again.

He decided to get in touch with Babi, to make sure she was all right, but there was no answer when he phoned. Then his tram arrived. He got on and glanced at his watch. Almost 9 p.m. He would visit her. It wasn't too late. Get back to the hotel first and pick up the car.

Snow was heaped up in giant piles in Babička's street. The ploughs had done their best. Now it was up to something else to finish the job; Spring, probably. He left the car at the end of the street and walked briskly along to the house. No need for stealth this time. The last thing George Mason would have now was time and resources to maintain surveillance.

There were no lights on in the house. Babi having an early night? He didn't want to disturb her. On the other hand, he knew she wouldn't mind him waking her up. Not at all. She would be avid for more news of Lisa.

He walked round the house, just to be sure. First impressions were right: no lights anywhere.

The spare key was still where it had always been kept, under a prominent stone in the garden. He collected it and rubbed off the damp soil, reminding himself to suggest it be placed inside a plastic bag in future.

At the front door, he hesitated before using the key, and then rang the bell. Opening the front door without warning might frighten her. Better to give her notice.

No one came to the door. He used the key and let himself inside. Then he switched on the hall light and called a greeting.

No response.

He called again, and listened. Nothing.

He moved on, switching on a couple more lights. Babička's bedroom on the ground floor was empty, the bed neatly made. He frowned, puzzled. Had she gone away? He wondered if some kindly friends had collected her and taken her to their cottage in the hills for a few days? That did happen from time to time.

The main living room was empty, too. And a lot tidier than it used to be, no doubt thanks to Lisa's departure.

He moved on again, and found her in the kitchen. She was in a heap on the floor. He stared, stupefied, and then let out a great roar of pain and anger. There was no need to check to make sure she was dead.

Chapter Twenty-Eight

She had been shot — eventually. When he calmed down enough to look closely, the bullet hole in the back of the head wasn't hard to find: the trademark execution. Before that, she had been knocked about. He could see that, too. The evidence was all over the kitchen.

They hadn't just come here to kill her. Whoever had done it had wanted something from her first. Information, presumably. She had nothing else to give. She didn't even have much of that. What could she have told them? Nothing. Almost nothing. She had no idea where he was, or where her granddaughter was. That was the reality. Prague or England would have been all she could have said. For that, she had paid a heavy price. A pointless killing, unless it was intended to anger or frighten him.

Jackson and Murphy, probably. It was their style. Utterly ruthless.

He turned away and considered his options. There weren't many. First, he had to get away from here. It went against the grain to abandon Babička like this, but he couldn't afford to be caught up in whatever happened next. He would be no use to Lisa, himself, or anybody else, if he was. It was as simple as that. He left.

Back at the car, he drove some distance away and then stopped to phone Mayhew.

'Something else has happened.'

'Go on.'

'Remember I told you about my daughter, and how she had been living with her grandmother here in Prague? Well, I've just found her grandmother – murdered.'

'By our mutual friend?'

'It looks like it. Him or his associated cretins.'

'I'm sorry, Harry. It's a sad situation. I wish there was something I could do.'

'I should have seen it coming,' Harry said bitterly, 'and done something to stop it.'

Mayhew didn't respond for a few moments. Then he said, 'Is there anything practical I can do to help you?'

'There is, yes. I don't want to get tied up with the police over this. Not now, anyway. It would be better if someone else could notify them of the death.'

'Of course. Give me the details.'

After he had been given the name and address, and a couple of other bits of information, Mayhew said, 'There is one thing I can tell you. We know a little more now about what Mason has been up to. We found one of his associates, and in exchange for the usual waivers he's told us the gist of it. Apparently, the elimination of Unit 89 was the price, or part of it, Mason agreed to pay for a significant stake for himself in a new gas field in Siberia. God knows who over there is in a position to make him such a gift, but that's what it all seems to be about.'

Confirmation, once again, that Mayhew had levelled with him. It was good to know. He toyed with the idea of telling Mayhew about Kuznetsov, but he dropped it. The time wasn't right.

'So I'm in his way?' he suggested.

'Exactly. Last man standing. As I said before, take care. He can't close the deal while you're still on your feet, and now he needs to do that more than ever. He's burned all his bridges with us.'

'At least I know where I stand,' Harry said, as if he hadn't until then.

Mulling it over on the drive back to Malá Strana, he swore bitterly as his thoughts returned to poor old Babička. What had she ever done to harm anyone? Nothing. Absolutely nothing at all. She was, had been, an extraordinarily good woman, and he had no idea how he would ever be able to tell Lisa what had happened to her. Damn Mason to hell!

Where was the bastard now? It had to be somewhere not far away. If Mason couldn't get to him and finish the job, then all that he had done so far would have been in vain. The killings and the loss of his career and country would have been for nothing, and the door closed on Siberian riches.

His guess was that Mason knew he was here, in Prague. They might have got enough out of Babička to make them believe that. Even if he wasn't, they might think that her death would bring him back. So Mason would probably be here too, somewhere, and still looking for him.

His thoughts turned to the Mason sighting near Lenka's place. Was it really him? He wasn't so sure now. It made little sense, for one thing. There was no reason for Mason to be in that area, no reason at all that he could see. If it had been him, it could only have been coincidence.

The worry that Lenka might be at risk had faded. Mason probably wouldn't even know she existed, still less have any reason to target her. Besides, he didn't do wet jobs himself. They were assigned to the likes of Jackson and Murphy. He must have been mistaken. It couldn't have been Mason.

Just as he reached the street where his hotel was located, the other possibility came to mind again. He swore, angry with himself for even thinking it. He must be going out of his mind. But he couldn't let it go. He parked along the street, and sat and brooded, unable to bring himself to get out of the car.

Lenka. Was she involved in some way he didn't know about? Was that why Mason might have been in the vicinity – to see her?

It didn't bear thinking about. But once raised, it was a question that wouldn't go away. He began to wonder if he had been incautious, naïve perhaps, in assuming Lenka was totally on his side. She had certainly helped him, but was that enough to prove her one-hundred per cent commitment to his cause?

Alternatively, once again, could Lenka herself be at risk? Perhaps Mason somehow knew she was helping him, and was set on eliminating her? It was a possibility, and one he liked better. He decided to speak to her again, and to warn her.

He started the car up and headed out to Strašnická. Late as it was, it would be better to speak to her face-to-face than risk using a phone.

He parked nearby and set off to walk to Lenka's apartment block. It was a beautiful night. Icy cold, no wind and a big, chilled moon that lit up a desolate landscape. Mountains of snow everywhere; cars still half-buried, not yet dug out. Just one car moving. It pulled to a stop outside Lenka's block. A man got out and headed for the entrance. The car moved away, with the soft purring sound that all big expensive cars make.

Harry blinked, gasped and began to run. He was too late. The entry door had opened and was shut again long before he reached it. By the time he arrived, the lift door, too, was closed and the lift was steadily ascending.

Through the dirty glass he watched the indicator button as the lift travelled upwards. It stopped at the seventh floor. Lenka's floor.

He pulled out his phone and hurriedly punched in the numbers. Come on, come on! he urged, almost demented, as the phone rang and rang. Eventually it was picked up.

'Lenka don't. . . .'

'Harry!'

She laughed and giggled at someone obviously close by.

'Lenka!'

But she wasn't in listening mode.

'Harry, you will never guess! I can't talk now. I am sorry. Stefan has just arrived. I am so excited!'

'What?'

'Stefan is here! He has been away so long. It is wonderful.'

'Are you all right?' he asked lamely.

She laughed.

'Marika's mother has been murdered, Lenka. I want you to be careful.'

'Oh? I am so sorry. But I must go now, Harry. I will phone you back later.'

Stefan, he thought, as he turned to walk away dejected. Yes, of course. Not George Mason at all. Or rather, it was. But he was also Stefan.

Chapter Twenty-Nine

It was a nightmare. No other word for it. But hadn't it been just that from day one? He swore savagely, started the engine and gunned it. Getting away from here was his priority now.

He drove aimlessly for hours. Only by driving fast on the empty night roads could he find distraction.

Lenka!

He didn't want to think about her, but ... her and Mason?

So she was involved. Somehow she was. He could be certain of that now. The best he could come up with was that her involvement was unwitting. Otherwise, surely, Mason would have found him by now – and she wouldn't have helped him in Vyšehrad anyway.

He wondered if she had also unwittingly given Mason information that had led to the death of Jan Klaus. He grimaced. Quite possibly. On the phone perhaps, she had casually told him where she was going, or where her friend was staying.

The reasoning made him feel slightly better. Perhaps Lenka was essentially innocent, even if she was involved. He didn't want to think any more about the possibility that she knew what she was doing, and had done all along.

Part of him longed now simply to turn the car west and

north, and drive until he reached The Running Man. But there was no way he could do that. Whatever was going on here had to be brought to an end before he left this time.

He grew tired, exhausted, and knew he had to stop before he fell asleep at the wheel. But he couldn't return to his hotel. He had to assume that Stefan, aka George Mason, was capable of finding it now he was back in town. Christ, all he had to do was ask Lenka!

He stopped finally on the edge of the city and booked into an all-night hotel, one with sparkling neon lights, lots of ladies in short skirts around and a steady stream of customers arriving and departing in Mercedes, BMWs and Audis. Most of the visitors were from over the border, the land of plentiful money and opportunity. He felt safe amid all the busy anonymity to get his head down and sleep.

In the morning, the car park was almost empty. No need to wonder why. He seemed to have been the only guest to have stayed more than a couple of hours. Even the dining room was deserted. Just as he was finishing a desultory breakfast, his phone rang. He picked it up and glanced at the screen. Lenka.

'Good morning, Harry! How are you today?'

He tried hard to cover his ambivalence. 'You sound happy?'

'Oh, yes. It is so good to have Stefan home again. Such a surprise, too. I wasn't expecting him yet.'

'Where has he been this time?'

'Russia, I think. I am not sure,' she said, laughing. 'It is always hard to pin him down, and to get him to remember exactly where and when he has been.'

Now there's a surprise! Harry thought.

'This time he has brought me some especially good news.

We have spoken in the past of retiring and moving out of Prague. Now, Stefan says, his business is going so well we can afford to do that. And I am ready for retirement.'

He grimaced. Retirement? On the proceeds from Siberian gas? Well, why not. Perfectly reasonable.

'Where would you go?' he asked. 'And where's Stefan from, for that matter?'

'Slovakia. That is the answer to both your questions. Somewhere peaceful in the mountains.'

He had wondered how Mason could get away with the language issue. He might well speak good Czech, but not like a native. The Slovaks, of course, had their own language. So not speaking Czech like a native wouldn't be a problem if you were a Slovak.

'Stefan speaks English, too,' she added. 'Very well, in fact.'

I just bet he does! Harry thought grimly.

'Often we find it is better for us to speak together in English, rather than Czech.'

He winced. God, Lenka! How naïve, how deluded, can you be?

'This evening, Harry, we would like to meet you and have dinner together. Is that possible, do you think?'

He was staggered. 'Aren't you too busy?' he asked lamely. 'I mean, if . . . Stefan has only just returned?'

'Oh, no! He insisted on meeting you when I told him about my old friend and colleague.'

'You didn't tell him too much, I hope?'

'No, of course not.' He heard her sigh with apparent regret. 'Unfortunately, there are limits to what I can confide to him.'

He shook his head. It just seemed to get worse.

'If you are agreeable,' Lenka continued, 'I would like to suggest we meet at a restaurant just the other side of Charles

Bridge.'

He thought quickly. Why not? This could be the opportunity he had been looking for. Get it over and done with.

'Yes,' he said slowly. 'It sounds a wonderful idea.'

Lenka suggested a time. And that was that. They would meet at the restaurant.

Afterwards, he returned to his room to think it through. The situation was different now, better in some ways, but a hell of a lot more complicated. He needed to get it right.

He didn't believe now that Lenka was part of the opposition, as briefly he had feared. It was far more likely that she was innocent, somehow duped by Mason. She didn't seem to be at risk herself at the moment either. That was another plus. But how the hell was he ever going to persuade her of Stefan's true identity? He soon dismissed that thought. He wasn't even going to try.

Another question he wasn't going to waste time on was how Mason and Lenka had got together in the first place. How the hell had that happened?

He couldn't remember Lenka ever having had a man in her life before. His assumption, Marika's too, was that she had no need of one. Well, somehow Mason had overcome that problem.

He must have had good reason to try, too. It was impossible to believe it was love, not for Mason. Lenka must have had something he needed, and needed very badly. Whatever that was, it was hard to see Lenka lasting long once he'd got it.

More immediately, of course, Lenka was giving Mason the chance to catch up with him. Once he had done that, he would be free to pick up his reward and walk away – from

Lenka and everything else.

Well, this evening would bring it all to a head. Harry didn't suppose either Lenka or he were intended to survive the night. But the evening would provide the chance he had been looking for, too. Showtime, he thought grimly. Showdown at the O.K. Corral. Bring it on!

Chapter Thirty

It was a long morning, and threatened to be a long day. Harry drove back to Malá Strana and parked the car. Then he set off to recce the restaurant.

He wondered what Mason's plan would be. Somehow he couldn't see any of them actually reaching the restaurant. All Mason needed was for him to approach the place, with Jackson and Murphy lying in wait. A quick double-tap from silenced weapons in a crowded street would take care of things, before they disappeared back into the shadows.

Mason wouldn't need to do anything himself; he could sit inside with Lenka, and fret with her over where her friend Harry Gibson was. No need at all to break cover at this point, unless his association with Lenka was no longer useful and he wanted rid of her.

For a moment, Harry wondered if instead of making plans like this he should simply tell Lenka who she was involved with, and put up with her anguish and disappointment, perhaps even total collapse. The trouble was, he didn't think he could do it; Lenka was in love. And he wasn't the man to douse the flame.

Possibly, just possibly, he might be able to convince her afterwards, but not in advance. Besides, he wanted Mason's plan to work – up to a point. He wanted the meeting to go ahead, not be aborted. This was the chance he had thought would never come. Tonight, at last, he could hit back.

Passing the buck to Mayhew was another option, and possibly a better one. He thought seriously about that. Would it work, though? What could Mayhew do? He was here on his own, with his own agenda, and faced with chaos at the embassy.

He could contact the Czechs. But that would lead him into a diplomatic nightmare: crazed British spies making mayhem on the streets of Prague! You could see the tabloid headlines now. Mayhew's career would be at an end, in all probability, and meanwhile Mason might well have been tipped off and got clean away.

All in all, Harry decided grimly, it was better to handle it himself – and make sure the job got done.

The restaurant Lenka had specified was small and discreet, in an historic street of churches, ancient houses, and bars and charming restaurants, all beneath the walls of the Hradčany castle. Harry stood in the doorway of a shop on the opposite side of the street and studied the approaches. At night it would be an excellent place for a stake-out. A narrow street, with dim lighting and vehicular restrictions, lots of tourists wandering by on foot, and plenty of doorways and shadows. Ideal. Hard to find a better ambush spot.

He guessed they would expect him to walk up from Charles Bridge, and look to waylay him before he reached the restaurant. So his best bet would be to come in from the other direction. Come down the hill from the castle. If he could reach the restaurant, he would hit Mason immediately, and take his chances thereafter. He doubted if Jackson and

Murphy would stick around with their boss dead.

It wouldn't be fun coping with Lenka. Quite possibly, she would turn on him. He shrugged; he would just have to deal with it. Somehow. Anyway, he still had a few hours to think about it. He left the doorway and set off to walk back towards Charles Bridge.

His phone vibrated with a text from Lenka. Change of plan, he read. The restaurant advised was not available tonight. Meet us at the end of Charles Bridge. We will walk together to another restaurant. Same time.

He smiled grimly. Well, the message might be from Lenka, but it might not. He didn't know who had been using Lenka's phone. It could have been Mason. This might be just a way of throwing him off course.

It could also be a way of cutting Lenka out of the loop, and creating a meeting she didn't even know about. If it was, it would be a change to welcome.

Keyed up, ready to go, he walked on.

Even on such a cold, dark evening, with piles of dirty snow everywhere, there were plenty of tourists about as he approached the huge archway that marked the entrance to Charles Bridge. He arrived early and slipped into the shadows, prepared to wait.

It was a long, cold wait, a full hour, to the appointed time. The crowds flowed past. Nearby, a sketch artist attracted a few customers, with his lightning cameos and cartoons. A little further along, a jazz band played Dixieland, while one man on his own sold atmospheric pictures of Old Prague and another worked the strings of a couple of wooden puppets that danced jerkily to music from his CD player.

The task he had set himself began to seem impossible.

How could he possibly pick out a Jackson or a Murphy, still less a George Mason, in all this noisy, moving mass of people?

He wondered what the plan might be. A knife between the ribs as the crowd pressed? A single, silenced shot fired at close quarters? Or even a push over the medieval ramparts of the bridge?

It wasn't good. He became restless, fearing he was not going to be able to cope with the threat, not here. Mason had too many options. The odds were stacked against him. He should walk away and think again. Arrange something more in his favour.

He pushed himself away from the wall, ready to leave. It was then that he saw Lenka. She was already here, and standing under the middle of the arch, exactly where they had arranged to meet. With her was a man he didn't know, had never seen before. Late thirties, perhaps. Tall and heavily built. Wearing a ski jacket and a woolly hat.

They were laughing and hugging one another, and clapping hands and stamping their feet to ward off the cold.

He stared. They seemed happy, very happy. Lenka turned and he saw from her face how happy she was. Stefan, obviously. Dear God! Don't say he had somehow managed to get it wrong after all?

For a moment he was too shocked to do anything but stare. He couldn't think. Then he took a deep breath and moved forward to greet Lenka.

'Been waiting long?' he asked, summoning a cheerful smile.

'Harry!' She laughed, surprised by his approach. 'Here you are. Not long, no.'

'And this must be Stefan?' he said, holding out his hand. 'Pleased to meet you at last.'

'No, no!' the newcomer said with a chuckle. 'I am Josef.'

'My brother,' Lenka added.

'Oh?' His heart missed a beat. He swung round to face Lenka. 'What about Stefan?'

'He will meet us at the restaurant. Come! Let us go.'

Her brother, he thought dully. Shit! Wrong again.

'Josef turned up unexpectedly, and I invited him to join us. I hope you don't mind?'

'No, of course not.'

He was back in high vigilance mode, his eyes scanning everyone within reach. How was this going to work? Where were they? He was back to Mason again, and to Jackson and Murphy. What did Lenka know? Anything? Was she still innocent?

'Do you live in Prague, Josef?'

'No. I live in Brno, in Moravia. So it is very rare that I get here to see my sister.'

They moved on, threading their way through the crowds, heading towards he had no idea what. Events had slipped out of his control. Mason was waiting somewhere, but where? And who was with him? And what did Lenka know?

'The two men in my life,' Lenka said gaily, 'and I hardly ever see them!'

He scarcely heard her.

Five minutes later, they reached the arch at the other end of Charles Bridge. He tensed. Not so many people on this side. But more shadows than ever. Beyond, a world of shadows, in the streets leading past the great churches and up to the castle. Surely it would be soon? He couldn't believe Mason would really wait until they reached the restaurant.

There was little traffic on the streets this side of the bridge. The odd parked car, but only the occasional vehicle actually moving. Evenings here belonged to the tourists, the people seeking the little bars and the restaurants in the historic huddle of ancient buildings below the castle and the cathedral.

So he immediately spotted the car that came round the corner at speed. He noticed, and stopped walking as it sped down the cobbled street towards them. He tugged Lenka's arm, urging her towards the sidewalk.

It was too late. As if in slow motion, he saw that the side window was down on the passenger side of the car. He saw the gun barrel poke out. And he saw the continual flashes as the assault weapon was fired, and felt and heard the swathe of bullets.

He saw Josef fall, and as he fell himself he felt Lenka sag away from him as she took bullets meant for him. Then the car was past, sliding on the damp cobbles and squealing round a corner.

People were screaming in the street. His hearing was fuzzy, but he heard them. His head was ringing and waves of agony distorted his vision, but his eyes began to clear. He realized then that he was on the ground, his face flat on the icy surface. He moved his head and saw he was lying next to Lenka. But it didn't feel real. Things were all wrong. Shock had him in its grip. People screaming!

He levered himself up into a sitting position as his senses began to return. He had been expecting an attack, but not one like this. He had been surprised and overwhelmed.

He scrabbled to his knees, knowing without thinking about it that he had not been hit. Lenka was face down, unmoving. He pulled her over onto her back, shouting at her to wake up. He touched her neck and could feel no pulse. He sought a pulse in other places, and couldn't find one.

Josef was groaning, alive still but not in good shape. A passer-by appeared alongside, and reached down to him with kind words. People were gathering. He could see their legs all around him.

Then he heard a huge bang and the squeal and grind of tortured metal from somewhere nearby. Round the corner, perhaps? He struggled to his feet and tottered in that direction.

A woman asked if he was all right. He ignored her and tried to run. Pain engulfed him, but he forced himself on.

Round the corner there was chaos. The car had slammed into a refuse truck making its evening round to empty street bins. The car had buried itself deep into the back of the truck. A man in a yellow safety jacket was flat on his back, motionless, in the middle of the street. Steam or smoke was rising from the wreckage. Other men in yellow jackets were closing in on the scene.

The passenger door of the car opened and a figure emerged, to hobble away. Mason. An attempt was made to detain him but gunshots sent two men to the ground. The rest backed off.

As he passed the car, Harry saw the lifeless figure of the driver trapped behind the steering wheel. He kept going, freeing his own gun as he ran. He called out Mason's name. The figure ahead of him turned and loosed off a fusillade of bullets from the assault weapon he was carrying.

Harry had dropped to the ground as he saw the gun coming round. Now he steadied the hand holding the Glock with his free hand and aimed carefully. He fired, once, twice. Mason stumbled and fell, and then squirmed and scrabbled to reach the weapon he had dropped. Harry got there first, and kicked it aside.

Someone nearby called his name. He spun round as two men converged on him, coming from he had no idea where.

'Harry!' one of them said again.

It was Kuznetsov.

'Yuri?'

The second man took his arm in a friendly way and steered him aside.

Kuznetsov smiled and stepped past. Harry followed him with his eyes, and saw him lean down and shoot Mason twice in the head.

'This way, Harry,' the man holding his arm said gently.

More dazed than ever, he allowed himself to be led away. Kuznetsov caught them up and took his other arm. Not far away, he heard the sound of approaching sirens. And possibly bells. He wasn't absolutely sure about the bells.

Chapter Thirty-One

They hustled him into a car parked nearby and drove away as flashing lights turned a corner and filled the street with carnival colours. Sirens suggested police cars were converging on the area from several directions.

'We had to get you away from there,' the other man said in heavily accented English. 'Sitting in a police cell for 48 hours while they sort out what has happened is no fun.'

Harry was sitting in the back of the car with the other man. Kuznetsov was driving.

'How are you feeling?' Kuznetsov called over his shoulder.

Harry grunted and just shook his head.

'Were you hit?' the other man asked.

'No,' he admitted.

'Shocked and dazed, probably. And a little battered and bruised, perhaps?' the other man said with a chuckle.

All of that, Harry thought miserably. He was still struggling to deal with Lenka's death and with what had happened to Mason.

Kuznetsov asked Harry if he had a car, and where it was. Then he drove him to where it was parked. On the way, he stopped to let the other man out.

'Before I disappear,' the man said, gripping Harry by the

arm hard, 'I want to tell you something very important. Mason will not trouble anyone again, obviously, but he has set something in motion that you must stop.

'His men, the two killers you know, are on their way to England. Their task is to abduct your daughter again. Mason is dead but they will not learn that for some time. They will carry on with their mission. You must stop them.

'Believe me, please, when I say that I wish none of this had happened. It is not my doing. But in a sense, I am responsible. I accept that.'

With that, he slid out of the door that Kuznetsov was holding open for him and faded into the night shadows.

Kuznetsov got back behind the wheel and they completed the journey to where Harry had parked his car.

'Who was he, Yuri?'

By then, he had recovered his senses.

Kuznetsov smiled. 'You don't need to know that, Harry.'

'Was it who I think it was?'

'What he said was true. You need to move fast, Harry. I hope you can manage it.'

'It was Kurst, wasn't it?'

'Perhaps.'

Kuznetsov sighed and added, 'He was not behind what Mason did. He wanted Mason in his pocket, it is true, because of his potential value in future. But not at any price.

'Once Mason had departed from his senses, and started taking desperate measures, he became a liability and was no longer of any value whatsoever. From then on, it became a matter of damage limitation.'

'But more damage still happened,' Harry pointed out bitterly.

Kuznetsov shrugged. 'It is true. I cannot deny it. But what he said to you is also true. You must hurry home, Harry. Here,' he added. 'This may help.'

He handed over a mobile phone. Harry looked at it.

'I took it from Mason,' Kuznetsov said. 'There may be information on it that you can use.'

Harry nodded his thanks.

'What are you doing here, Yuri? This isn't your fight.'

Kuznetsov smiled. 'Maybe I will see you in London, Harry,' he said mysteriously.

'Working for Kurst?'

'Who knows?'

Kuznetsov held out his hand. Harry took it. Belatedly, he thought of a question he still hadn't asked.

'How did you and Kurst happen to be there, on the spot?' he asked. 'How did you know what was going to happen this evening?'

Kuznetsov chuckled. 'You expect me to tell you all my trade secrets, Harry?'

Harry shook his head. 'I would have shot him again myself if you hadn't turned up.'

'Maybe; maybe not. We wanted to make sure. Believe me Harry, it was for the best.'

Perhaps it was, Harry thought, as he watched Kuznetsov drive away. He wasn't really certain he could have found it in him to shoot a badly injured man.

'Mayhew? Mason's dead.'

There was a brief pause.

'Can you tell me more?'

'It's a long story. I was with a couple of people when he tried a drive-by shooting. He got two hits but missed me.

Then his vehicle crashed, and. . . . Well, you can guess the rest.'

'I really will need detail, you know.'

'I'll let you have it, but not now. I have to go. I've learned his two hitmen are after my daughter again. I must get to her before they do.'

Mayhew was quiet for a heartbeat. Then he said, 'Anything I can do?'

'Not for me directly. But you may need to smooth over some serious wrinkles. One of the people with me was a Czech intelligence officer, a friend, who has been helping me. She was killed. The man with her was her brother from Brno. He was also hit. I don't know if he survived.'

'I see.'

Harry took a deep breath and added, 'Sadly, and unknown to me, the woman was in a relationship with Mason, who she knew as "Stefan". It must sound complicated, but that's how it was. I'll tell you more another time.'

'Thank you. Get back to me when you can.'

Thank God for cold efficiency, Harry thought with relief after he had switched off. Mayhew was just what he needed right now. No questions that would have the effect of holding him up.

He turned the ignition key and started up, and pointed the car towards the airport on the outskirts of the city. There was nothing he could do for Lenka or her brother. His priority was clear: to get back home ASAP.

He kept all his questions and doubts at bay until he was on the plane and could think properly about them. It would have been Lisa's phone call to Babi that had told them where she was, he decided. They must still have been monitoring

Babi's phone.

So Lisa's innocent call had resulted in Babi's needless murder, and Mason knowing where Lisa was. He grimaced. A terrible price had already been paid unwittingly by a little girl anxious to speak to her grandmother. He had to hope he could stop the price rising still higher.

Two hours, he thought. That's how long the flight to Newcastle would be. Then another hour, say, to get to The Running Man. Would it be enough?

Chapter Thirty-Two

The mobile Kuznetsov had given him told him a lot of what he needed to know. Until he examined it he was floundering in the dark, but on the flight he had plenty of time to read the texts and listen to the voicemails.

The plan was straightforward: Jackson and Murphy were to take their car to the village of Granton in Northumberland. There, they were to look for Gibson's daughter, and take her. They were given the number of the phone she had used in calling her grandmother. The child was to be taken to somewhere called Košice – which Harry knew to be in Slovakia – where they could collect their financial package, as previously agreed.

Harry wondered if Košice had just been a transit point for Mason. Surely he would have had to move on? To somewhere in Russia, perhaps? That would have been just about the only country where Mason could have felt safe. He smiled. Mason could have led a great life there, in Siberia probably, counting his money.

A couple of things stood out. One, the instruction was to abduct, not kill, Lisa. Presumably as insurance, a bargaining counter. That was something to be grateful for, he supposed, although it was hard to see how she could have survived the ordeal planned for her. He knew hostages had a poor life expectancy, especially when crossing international borders.

Two, it was clear that Mason and the others had planned to split up and go their own ways after this. It was tempting to wonder what Jackson and Murphy would do now if they knew Mason was dead. Abort? Take off? Disappear? That might depend on whether they would still be able to pick up their money with Mason dead. They could be stuck, out on a limb, with nothing to show for their work for him.

He wondered what they would say, and do, if he phoned them now on Mason's phone and told them their boss was dead. Laugh in his face, probably. They would take some convincing.

Mayhew might be able to do it, of course. That was a better idea. He might even be able to offer them some sort of immunity to persuade them to abandon their mission and walk away.

That thought wasn't especially appealing; Jackson and Murphy walk free? No retribution for murdering Babička and the men in Unit 89? No way!

On the other hand, he liked the thought of them getting close to Lisa even less. Priorities, he thought. Be practical, and realistic. These were desperate, dangerous men, and he was one man alone who was not in their class as a killer.

He considered the timetable. The latest message on Mason's phone suggested Jackson and Murphy had set off at about ten that morning. Even if they drove non-stop, sharing the driving, he couldn't see them getting to north Northumberland before six or seven o'clock in the morning. So there was time to set something up.

He tapped his fingers on the armrest until the man next to him looked up from his Kindle and frowned. He apologized and got up to head for the toilet. Once inside, he took out his phone and made the call.

'Yes, Harry?'

'Hi. I'm flying to Newcastle. I've just been going through the messages on Mason's mobile, working out their plan. I'm hoping you might be able to intercept Jackson and Murphy before they can do what they've been sent to do.'

'Tell me.'

He told Mayhew what he knew, and what he guessed. He also told him what he didn't know and couldn't guess.

'So you think they can't arrive before about seven or eight in the morning?'

'That's my best estimate.'

'Right. What car are they using?'

'No idea, I'm afraid.'

'Don't worry. Leave it to us. We'll check the ferries and Eurostar. I'm sure we'll be able to stop them.'

Harry switched off as someone started hammering on the toilet door. He got up and made his exit.

'Are you all right, sir?' a stewardess asked.

'Yes, thanks. And, no, I wasn't smoking in there,' he added with a smile.

She didn't look amused.

So leave it to Mayhew, he thought with relief. He had plenty of resources to call on back in the UK. It was much more sensible than trying to do everything himself.

He had called Ellie earlier and asked her if she could get someone to pick him up at the airport. She was waiting for him herself when he came out of Arrivals.

He smiled. 'You're a sight for sore eyes!' he said, taking

her in his arms.

She held on to him for a moment and looked up. He kissed her and then turned her towards the exit.

'No luggage?'

He shook his head.

'And no car.' She stared at him and added, 'Trouble?'

'I'm afraid so.'

On the way, he tried to summarize everything that had been happening, and where things stood now. It was a lot for her to take in, he knew, even in condensed form, but he had to do it. At least she didn't throw up her hands and scream at him to get out of the car.

'Poor Lisa,' she said when he broke off. 'And poor you!' He thought she was done, but then she added, 'I thought it must be something like that.'

'You did?' He was surprised.

'Spies, and things.'

'Mostly things,' he said quietly. 'We haven't been doing much spying for a long time, and I'm out of it now anyway.'

'You sure?'

He nodded. 'Certain.'

His phone rang when they were about halfway back to the village. He pulled it out and glanced at it. Mayhew.

'Yes?'

'I'm sorry to tell you this, Harry, but we were too late. We just missed them.'

His heart seemed to miss a beat.

'Where?' he asked, wondering if they were on a ferry. 'Calais?'

'Dover, as well. They're moving fast. They're in the

country, and presumably heading your way.'

He grimaced.

Mayhew continued, 'They are travelling in a black Jaguar – or they were. Helped themselves to embassy property once again.'

'They need to change the locks in that place.'

'Don't they just? We'll do what we can, of course, and no doubt catch up with them eventually, but I wanted you to be on guard.'

'Thanks.'

He switched off and thought furiously. Either they were ahead of schedule or they had started off earlier than he had believed.

He glanced at his watch. Midnight plus ten now. Five or six hours before they arrived? Something like that. He needed to move Lisa out of harm's way.

'It's not over, after all, is it?' Ellie said quietly.

'I'm afraid not.'

'What needs doing?'

'There are two men coming for Lisa. We need to move her away from the hotel to somewhere safe.'

'Because the hotel was where she made the phone call from?'

'That's right.'

'What else needs doing?'

'Let's just concentrate on that for the moment. We need to move her, in case we can't stop them coming.'

'Who is *we*?'

'That was a very senior officer in MI6 that just called me. He will be doing what he can to have these men intercepted long before they can reach Northumberland.'

Ellie digested that for a moment. He was amazed she was

so calm. This was an extraordinary intrusion into her life. She was doing very well.

'Any ideas about where we might take her?' he asked gently. 'I know it's difficult at a moment's notice, especially at this time of night, but it's got to be done. If necessary, I'll take her camping.'

'No need for that.' Ellie pondered a moment and then said, 'I'll take her to my mother's. She lives just outside the village.'

That sounded good to him.

'What will you do?' she asked.

'Belt and braces!' he said cheerfully. 'I'm going to position myself strategically, in case MI6 can't do the job.'

Back at The Running Man, he lifted Lisa from her bed and silently swept her away to the car, Ellie following with an extra quilt to wrap her in. The little girl didn't wake up. He was glad of that. More explanation, especially to Lisa, would have been beyond him just then.

The journey was one of only a few minutes. Surprisingly, a light was still shining in the cottage of Ellie's mother.

'Oh, she doesn't sleep much these days,' Ellie said. 'She'll love having a visitor, as well. Give me a minute with her, and then bring Lisa in.'

It worked. A few minutes and they were out of there, and back in the car. One problem dealt with, Harry thought with relief.

'Can I borrow the car?' he asked.

'Wouldn't the Land Rover be better? It's just round the back of the hotel.'

'Perhaps it would. Thanks.'

He hesitated then. There was something else he needed,

but he doubted very much if Ellie could help with that. Still, he had to ask.

'The Running Man is an old hunting lodge, isn't it?'

'It was once,' she said, glancing at him.

'I don't suppose there might be any ... weapons laid around anywhere, would there?'

'Firearms, you mean?'

'Well. . . .'

'There's a shotgun you can have, and a box of cartridges. My father's,' she added before he asked.

'Oh?'

'Everyone in the country used to have a shotgun,' she said. 'It didn't used to be like it is now.'

Less dangerous, probably, he thought. They wouldn't ever have had people like Jackson and Murphy arriving on their doorstep.

Back at the hotel, he took delivery of the shotgun and the keys to the Land Rover.

'Take care,' Ellie said, sounding, and looking, troubled.

'I will.'

'Can I ask where you're headed?'

He hesitated. But she deserved an answer.

'To where the road from the A1 climbs that first hill. If they get that far, I'll catch them there.'

Chapter Thirty-Three

He was impatient to get moving and gunned the Land Rover hard. It leapt forward, as if it had been waiting all its life to be part of some kind of emergency. As he left the village he flipped on the high beams and floored the accelerator. It was ten or fifteen miles to the junction where the road to the village left the A1. Quarter of an hour, he hoped.

The road wound its way through dark and dripping woodland. No snow yet in this part of the world, but plenty of winter rain. The tarmac shone bright in his headlamps and the surface was slick with water and fallen leaves. He slowed down; no point going so fast he ended up in a ditch.

He wondered what they would do, how they would make their approach. So far as he knew, the road he was taking was the only way into the village. There would be other approaches, no doubt. Single-lane tarmac strips and rough tracks over the hills. But anyone reaching this part of the world having driven the best part of a thousand miles straight off, and arriving in the middle of the night in unknown territory, probably wouldn't be looking for roads that were not on the satnav or whatever road atlas they were using. Their aim would be to get here, get the job done and get the hell out fast – in the unlikely event of them evading

Mayhew's hounds.

His mind ran ahead to the turn-off from the A1. Flat land there, for a mile or so; fields surrounded by low hawthorn hedges. Difficult to surprise them there, if they ever got this far. Better to come inland a mile or so, to where the river wound through the hills, and the road ran high up on the hillside.

If he remembered rightly, there was a spot where you could see a little way down the road, and see what was coming. It was right on the edge of woodland, too: that would be a good place to wait.

He might not need to do anything at all, of course, he reminded himself yet again. It was unlikely that Jackson and Murphy would be able to travel the length of the country in an official car without being spotted and stopped. Mayhew would be exerting all his considerable influence on this one.

So all he was, really, was backup. He was the last-ditch defence, in case the improbable happened. He needed to be there, just in case. Lisa was his daughter. To Mayhew, her abduction or death would be unfortunate and regrettable; to him, it would be the end of the world. So he would wait until either Mayhew called to say it was over, or he saw Jackson and Murphy coming down the road.

He parked on a corner, on a patch of rough ground just off the road, where the highway authority stored a heap of grit for when the ice and snow came. Then he checked his phone. Nothing from Mayhew, or from anyone else.

He checked his watch next: 1.45 a.m. Going to be dark for the next five or six hours. Perhaps even longer, given the cloud cover and spasmodic rain. That meant any vehicle approaching from the A1 would have its lights on. He would see it in good time. If it did come to that, his plan was to block the road with the Land Rover – and fight it out. Not very sophisticated, but it probably wasn't going to happen anyway.

No good sitting here, he soon decided. He couldn't see much of the road. He was going to have to get out and get wet. In the back of the Land Rover, he found a big plastic sheet and a rug that smelled as if it had known dog. He took them both. He needed anything he could find to keep the weather off him, and to keep the shotgun dry. A last look round. Then he got out and made his way to the corner, where he found a vantage point overlooking the road coming from the east. He settled down there to wait.

He positioned himself in the lee of a big boulder, trees on either side and above and behind to keep off some of the wind and rain. Under the plastic sheet it was dry enough but noisy. The plastic crackled with every little movement and the raindrops hitting it sounded like drumbeats.

It was stormy for an hour. Then the wind dropped and the rain stopped. The sky cleared a little. In places he could see stars. He pushed the plastic sheet back from his head with relief.

In the distance, he could see a constant stream of traffic using the A1, but no vehicle had turned onto the road he was watching. One time, he fancied he heard a vehicle engine labouring up a slope, but nothing came his way from either direction and he decided his ears were playing tricks. The constant dripping of raindrops from the surrounding trees made it difficult to identify any other sound.

He was cold and for a time had to fight off sleep as well. Much as he was determined to stay vigilant, it was hard to do. He resorted to little tricks and manoeuvres he had learned over the years. Push-ups increased the blood flow and brought warmth. Counting to a thousand, breaking and then doing it again stopped him glancing at his watch every minute or two.

He tried to identify the sounds he could hear on all sides now the wind and the rain had eased away. There were creatures out here with him, even if he couldn't see them. Small things that moved swiftly in little bursts of energy, and something bigger that was less worried about being noticed. Deer? Badger? Maybe a fox? It didn't matter. The unseen citizens of the night helped keep him alert.

Just after 5 a.m. his phone buzzed. Mayhew. News?

'No, nothing, I'm afraid,' Mayhew said. 'I guessed you would be up, and just thought I'd let you know. It's not good, I know, but we'll get them.'

Maybe, Harry thought afterwards. Maybe they would. But the doubts were beginning to grow. He was glad he was here, not in a warm bed in The Running Man. He wondered if Mayhew had called partly to keep himself awake. The man had been on the go a long time now without much sleep, if any. It was one of those times when the intelligence community didn't work office hours, not even at Mayhew's level.

Now the small hours were well past, Harry realized his own sleepiness had gone. He was tired but more awake. He glanced up at the sky, wondering how long it would be before a hint of light appeared in the east. Another couple of hours, probably.

He was right about that. Just after 7 a.m. he fancied he could see a lighter patch in the sky, just a faint suggestion that the blackness was beginning to fade. Then, as if on cue, he saw a vehicle turn off the A1 and onto the road to the village. He got to his feet. He had no idea what it was, but it was the first vehicle he had seen.

It was still utterly dark down below where he stood. He watched the vehicle's steady progress for a full minute, still undecided what it was. Then he leapt round and slid down to where he'd parked.

The Land Rover started first go. He reversed it in a wide swing that took it out across the road, and blocked it. Then he pulled on the handbrake, switched off the ignition and got out. He moved into the trees at the side of the road, and waited. If the oncoming vehicle was innocent, he would just have to move the Land Rover and suffer the angry complaints, always assuming there wasn't an almighty smash.

But it was the Jaguar. It rounded the corner and screeched to a stop.

There was a moment when nothing happened, and all was utter silence. Then doors opened. Jackson got out, looked around and leaned down to say something. Murphy got out.

'That's far enough!' Harry called. 'Stand still.'

Jackson wheeled round and opened fire with a pistol he was holding.

Harry pulled the trigger on the shotgun and blasted heavy-duty shot at them. Jackson was hit. He staggered, but stayed upright, and made it round the back of the car into shelter. Harry fired again. Then he reloaded and shifted position. Murphy spotted his movement and opened fire.

It was almost stalemate. Harry knew he couldn't hit them while they were behind the car. Nor could they go anywhere without exposing themselves to his fire. Behind them, there was a narrow strip of tarmac and verge, and then the ground fell away in a precipitous drop to the river. In the dark, they couldn't escape that way.

Their best bet, he thought, would be to try a pincer movement. If Murphy went one way and Jackson the other, both maintaining fire, one of them might get across the road and behind him. Would they risk it? How badly was Jackson hit? Was he capable of taking part?

Almost stalemate. Then, while he was reloading again, something else came into the equation. He heard the boom of a powerful weapon fired from somewhere overhead. The Jag rocked with the impact of heavy-calibre bullets.

Within moments, Jackson and Murphy had reassessed the situation. In the growing light, Harry saw movement and heard the engine starting up. One of them got the car into reverse, and it started screaming backwards at speed. Harry fired and saw the windscreen explode. The Jag kept going. He fired again. It kept going.

Then the other weapon spoke once more and the car lurched and changed tack, as a tyre was blown off the rim. It spun round, kept going, plunged over the edge of the road and disappeared.

For a moment, there was the sound of an engine racing right off the monitor. Then came the sound of something very heavy crashing through trees, smashing branches and trunks, bouncing off the rocky slope and finally, thundering into the earth a couple of hundred feet below. An explosion followed and a ball of light lit up the morning sky.

Harry was stunned. For a moment, he simply stared, and listened. Then he got shakily to his feet and looked up at the hillside behind him. Had one of Mayhew's people managed to get here in time?

He saw and heard nothing, and there was no way up there in the dark. Instead, he turned back and ran across the road to look down into the gully.

The Prague embassy was one Jag down. What was left of all that expensive metal and plastic was a huge fireball, resting down near the river, broken trees indicating the route it had taken to get there. It was a safe bet that no one had got out.

'Did we get them?' a woman's voice called to him.

He spun round and gaped. 'Jesus, Ellie! Where the hell. . . ? Was that you up there?' he asked, incredulous, seeing the rifle she was holding.

'It's Dad's old hunting rifle,' she said, glancing at it. 'He always said he wanted me to learn how to use it, as it might come in handy one day. I guess he was right.'

Harry shook his head, in awe of the woman standing before him. She walked towards him. He took hold and hugged her.

'How on earth did you get here?' he asked.

'I thought you might need help,' she said. 'But I didn't want to distract you.'

He chuckled with amazement and relief.

'So,' she added, 'I took a forestry road that brings you out up above where I knew you were going to wait.'

'God, Ellie!' he said, hugging her hard. 'You did so well. I can't believe it!'

'It was worth the wait, wasn't it?'

There was no denying that.

'What about down there?' she added, motioning towards the gully.

'Nothing we can do, or that I would want to do. Let the police sort it out tomorrow. I'll just give the boss man a call, and let him know what's happened here.'

'Are you going to tell him we've done his job for him?'

'I just might, at that,' Harry said with a grin.

Chapter Thirty-Four

He watched Lisa playing in the garden behind the hotel. He sat down and watched her without calling to her. A dog was with her, a Border collie of Ellie's that seemed as bright and athletic as Lisa herself.

When she turned and saw him, she looked stunned for a moment. Then her face broke out into a million smiles. She gave a little shriek and started running towards him. The dog watched, briefly puzzled, and then raced after her joyously.

'Daddy, you're home!'

'Hello, sweetheart!' He laughed and swept her up in his arms. 'Yes, I'm back home – for good this time.'

Home, though? Was that the right word?

Then he caught sight of Ellie heading towards them with a tray of drinks. Yes, he decided happily. Home was exactly the right word.

He spoke once or twice by phone to Mayhew, tying up loose ends, accepting the need for some sort of debriefing.

'We need to look at ourselves,' Mayhew said, 'and that's what I'll do when I get back to London. There's no way Jackson and Murphy should have been able to make a journey like that without us stopping them.'

'They got lucky,' Harry said mildly.

'Until the very end, from what I hear. Then their luck ran out altogether. A pity, really. I would have liked the opportunity to debrief them.'

Harry was having none of it. They had met a bad end, but they had caused bad ends for too many people he knew for him to be upset about that.

'Did you find anything more about who Mason did the deal with?' he asked cautiously, curious to know how far Mayhew had got with his enquiries.

'Only up to a point. We're still working on that. We believe it started with one of the émigrés while Mason was working in London. As to who, ultimately, was behind it, who knows? We may find out, or we may not. Russia is still an opaque country to us, as you must know as well as anyone.'

Yes indeed, Harry thought. Anywhere as big and complex as Russia was bound to be hard to fathom. Give him the Czech Republic any day!

He said nothing about Kurst. Or Kuznetsov. Without their intervention, the story would have ended very differently. They had helped him, and he was grateful to them. He wouldn't risk compromising them. His loyalties were more nuanced now than they had been in the past.

'You were right about Mason being shacked up with the Czech woman, by the way,' Mayhew added. 'His assistant has confirmed that.'

'Has he told you why, or how, it happened?'

'More or less. Mason wanted to locate Unit 89 members even before he knew Landis was onto him. But Callerton had set things up so that the team was unknown to the embassy. Mason knew you existed, of course, but not where you were located. He thought the Czechs probably knew where you were, though. So he targeted what he believed was a weak link in their outfit.'

'Novotná?'

'Yes, Novotná. He believed he could find you through her.'

Harry grimaced. In a sense, Mason had been proved right, but due more to luck than anything else. Lenka had been no weak link. Just in the wrong place at the wrong time. Like the rest of us, he thought sadly.

'And you haven't changed your mind?' Mayhew added. 'You're still intent on resigning?'

'I already did,' Harry said, managing a wry chuckle. 'I'm out of it now.'

'Then good luck for the future.'

No attempt to dissuade him, Harry thought afterwards with approval. Mayhew was too good at his job to want to pursue lost causes.

'Just let me get this straight,' Ellie said thoughtfully. 'This man, Mason, had your team assassinated, murdered, because. . . ?'

'Because he knew that our contact man, John Landis, was about to tell us and London what he'd discovered.'

'Which was? I know you've told me once,' she hastened to add, 'but tell me again.'

'Mason had made a deal with certain London-based, Russian business interests – oligarchs, if you like. In return for a small share in a new Siberian gasfield, Mason would be their man inside MI6.

'But Mason knew that if London found out about this he would no longer be of value to the Russians. The deal would be taken off the table. He couldn't allow that to happen.'

'So he took action to stop it.'

Harry nodded.

Ellie got up to move the tray of drinks closer and pour them both refills. He watched her intently. She did every-thing so elegantly. He loved watching, and being near her.

When she sat down again, she said, 'It was a bit drastic, wasn't it?'

He shrugged agreement, and tried to explain – as much as he could understand Mason's perverse thinking.

'The deal on offer was very important to him. Mason was a disappointed man. He hadn't got the job he believed should have been his, and the job he did have was being down-graded. He would be made redundant and forced into early retirement.

'His career was coming to an end, with very little to show for it. He resented that. So he decided to look to his own interests. When Kurst approached him with an offer, he jumped at it.'

Ellie thought it over. 'But it wasn't the Russians who elim-inated your team?'

He shook his head. 'That was all Mason's own work. The Russians have been helpful, actually – both their secret service and the oligarchs in London. They didn't want us dead, and once they knew what was happening they were as interested as anybody in stopping Mason. He had become a mad dog.'

Ellie stood up again and reached for the coffee jug she had brought along with the long, cool drinks. Then she paused, jug in hand, as a new thought came to her.

'Would Mason have been a rich man, if things had worked out for him?'

'Very.' He thought for a moment and added, 'Colossally

rich, probably.'

'Harry,' she said wistfully, 'have you ever thought of contacting those people – those oligarchs?'

'Too late,' he said with a grin. 'I'd be no good to them now. I've resigned.'

There was one other thing Mayhew had told him that Harry pondered and felt glad about. Although Lenka had not survived Mason's attack, her brother somehow had. He was now back home in Brno recuperating. In time, Harry felt, he would mourn Lenka properly and visit Brno to see Josef. But not just yet. The wounds, for both of them, were still too fresh.

So this is my new life, he thought wonderingly, looking around the garden at the back of the hotel. Lisa had her arms around the dog, which kept making half-hearted attempts to wash her face with his tongue. And without looking, he knew Ellie was by his side. He could feel her presence all around him. He reached out, took hold of her hand and felt her smile.